WINTER'S WIDOW
THE WICKED WINTERS BOOK 12

SCARLETT SCOTT

Winter's Widow

The Wicked Winters Book 12

All rights reserved.

Copyright © 2021 by Scarlett Scott

Published by Happily Ever After Books, LLC

Edited by Grace Bradley

Cover Design by Wicked Smart Designs

This book or any portion thereof may not be reproduced or used in any manner whatsoever without the express written permission of the publisher except for the use of brief quotations in a book review.

The unauthorized reproduction or distribution of this copyrighted work is illegal. No part of this book may be scanned, uploaded, or distributed via the Internet or any other means, electronic or print, without the publisher's permission. Criminal copyright infringement, including infringement without monetary gain, is punishable by law.

This book is a work of fiction and any resemblance to persons, living or dead, or places, events, or locales, is purely coincidental. The characters are productions of the author's imagination and used fictitiously.

For more information, contact author Scarlett Scott.

www.scarlettscottauthor.com

CHAPTER 1

*A*s had become a nightly ritual, Lady Fortune was brimming with London's wealthiest and finest females in search of diversion. Perfumed and powdered, masked and bang up to the mark in exquisite gowns, and each of them ready to wager their pin money or their husband's fortunes on the next turn of a card.

It was a beautiful sight to behold.

Demon Winter circled one of the faro tables at his sister Gen's exclusive ladies' gaming hell, on his way to the private room where a patron had requested to meet him. He was well accustomed to the lingering stares and longing looks the club members sent his way. But this—a demand to meet with him alone—was new. In truth, the lady in question—*number one hundred four*, by club records—had asked for the owner of Lady Fortune.

But as the bride to the Marquess of Sundenbury and a future duchess, Gen was keeping her identity as the owner of Lady Fortune a closely guarded secret. Which meant Demon would be meeting with *number one hundred four* instead of

Gen. It was a nuisance he had not needed on a night that was already laden with problems.

The Madeira shipment was late.

Their resident scamp Davy had been caught filching a fan from *number two-and-twenty*.

Gen's new pup had shat in the kitchens, much to the outrage of their chef.

Demon sighed, then forced a smile in the direction of a brunette lovely who was attempting to catch his eye. At first, becoming the face of Gen's gaming hell had seemed a rum lark. Leave his position at The Devil's Spawn, a men's gaming hell, for an establishment overrun with ladies? Hardly a sacrifice.

However, there were nights like this one when Lady Fortune lost its bleeding luster.

Another few steps brought him to the door which led to Lady Fortune's private rooms, where its patrons could clandestinely engage in games with higher stakes. Or take dinner or tea. Whichever they preferred.

He reached the first private room, knocking before entering.

"Come," called an unfamiliar voice from within.

Number one hundred four was unknown to him. A relatively new patron.

Demon opened the portal, then crossed the threshold, closing it discreetly behind. Her back was to him, giving him a unique vantage point. In the low, intimate light of the room, her copper hair shone from its confinement in an elegant chignon. Her neck was creamy and elegant, enhanced by a golden necklace. Her shoulders were bare, making his gaze catch on one of his favorite places on a woman's body—that secret space where her neck and her shoulder met.

She turned, and his breath caught. For a moment, his

annoyance fled. Even obscured though much of her countenance was by a gold mask, she was beautiful.

"Sir."

"My lady." He bowed.

Demon Winter may have been born in the rookeries, but he knew what was expected from him by the quality.

She curtseyed, and it was then that he noticed the tremble —albeit slight—in her gloved hands. "Thank you for agreeing to an audience with me."

He nodded, wanting her to get the bloody hell on with it. "Of course, my lady. It's my duty to make certain the members of Lady Fortune are well pleased."

Pink stole across her cheeks.

Fancy that, a lady who flushed. Interest flared despite himself. He had not intended those words the way she had interpreted them, but somehow, it no longer seemed to matter.

"So I have been told," she said, her blue gaze dropping to the floor, as if she were afraid to hold his stare for too long.

He found himself drawing nearer to her without realizing what he was about. She smelled bloody good, like something rare, floral, and exotic. He wondered where she applied the scent. Behind her ears? The hollow of her throat? Her inner wrist?

The possibilities were as endless as they were delicious.

Oh, what the hell was he thinking? He needed to rid himself of *number one hundred four* so he could make Davy clean up dog shit.

Demon stopped short of her. He knew his boundaries. "How can I help you, my lady? Say the word, and it shall be yours."

She wetted her lips with her tongue, then inhaled sharply. "I am in need of your assistance."

His assistance? The petticoats at Lady Fortune were an

interesting blend of dedicated sinners and bored women in search of entertainment. They had made all manner of requests thus far—hothouse pineapple, gin to supplement the Madeira, lewd publications, and the list went on. Never, however, had anyone asked him for assistance until now.

Demon could not deny he was intrigued. "I am listening."

She hesitated. "The matter is...a delicate one."

"What matter isn't?" he asked, impatience growing.

The evening had only just begun, and already, he had tarried here too long, tempted by a lady he had no business being drawn to. Gen had made it clear as a window pane that the members of her establishment were not his for the tupping.

Her lips—a full, lush mouth, he noted, made for kissing—tightened in displeasure. "Indeed."

He was not telling her what she wished to hear. That much was apparent. But how was he to know what the devil she wanted? Standing there, looking so lovely, smelling so damned delicious. Tempting him.

Christ. He had no doubt Gen would tattoo his face in his sleep if he attempted to bed any of her fancy clientele. He had to force the woman to bloody well spill whatever it was she needed to tell him so he could carry on with the evening.

"What do you have need of, my lady?" he asked, impatient. "If it is a fruit or some such you're after, I will request it from the kitchens. If it's a game, I'll have it brought to the floor. If it's—"

"None of those things, sir," she interrupted, her body as stiff as an icicle hanging from the eaves, her voice just as cold.

"I'm not a soothsayer," he returned. "Before I can give you what you want, I need to know what it is you're after."

"This was an error on my behalf. Forgive me for importuning you." Her voice had softened, and he thought he detected a tremble in her chin. "I told Octavia coming here was a mistake."

The last, she muttered to herself.

The woman grew more fascinating by the moment.

"It's my pleasure to see to the happiness of all Lady Fortune's members," he said, trying for a bit of gallantry and thinking Gen would be proud. "Don't know who Octavia is, but I'm sure you being here isn't a mistake."

"Never mind who Octavia is." She caught her skirts in her gloved hands and moved to swish past him, dudgeon high. "I was wrong to seek you out."

He should allow this mysterious, alluring woman to go. Let her disappear into the fabric of Lady Fortune, where the sea of masked ladies rendered each indistinguishable from the next. And yet, Demon caught her elbow as she made to pass him.

She stopped, turning toward him. Her eyes, the deepest shade of blue he had ever seen, cut straight to the heart of him.

He almost forgot himself, forgot it was *he* who had halted her. "I am here now, my lady. There is no need to run."

Her chin went up. "I am not running."

He dared to counter her. "Looks like you were trying to, doesn't it?"

What was the matter with him? He was not meant to defy the patrons. Gen would punch him in the eye if she knew.

Bloody good thing Gen didn't know. She was in Mayfair this evening. Far from the edge of the East End, this meeting of realms where London's elite came to play in decadence amongst the lords of the underworld.

"Secrecy is essential," she said.

The warmth of her was seeping into him, so he released her, disliking the effect she had upon him. How long had it been since he had last bedded a woman? Too long. He would have to rectify that. Soon, if the tightening of his trousers had anything to say about it.

"Upon my honor," he reassured the masked lady who had sought him out.

She didn't need to know he possessed scarcely any honor. He had what little his father had bestowed upon him. Curse Papa Winter to his lecherous soul.

Still, she hesitated, looking torn. "You do not know who I am?"

"*Number one hundred four.*" His response was easy—that was all she was to him. All she could be.

Gen had developed an ingenious system for her membership, which had led to its rapid growth. The ladies were guaranteed their privacy. Each was assigned a number and nothing more. They entered Lady Fortune wearing masks and left wearing them. The ladies loved it—from the private gaming hell that was theirs alone, to the assurance their secrets were safe.

She rolled her lips, taking longer than necessary to answer him once more. At last, she spoke.

"I require a lover."

Well, *hell*.

That was decidedly not what he had been expecting. At all. Also, would it be wrong to suggest himself for the position?

Demon could not stay the swift thought, but he promptly dashed it. Gen would kick him in the arse.

"Here now." He frowned. "I ain't a pimp."

Damn it—there went his efforts at speaking like a gentleman. He had been working on his unchecked tongue so well thus far.

"It was not my intention to suggest you were."

He stroked his jaw, considering her, enjoying her feminine curves in that gown far more than he ought. "Explain, madam."

"This club's attraction is its secrecy and circumspection."

Was it?

"Hmm. I thought it was the hazard tables," he said lightly, as if they were equals.

There was something about this moment between them that was personal. Intimate. *Carnal*, even. The air seemed charged and ready to combust. Or mayhap that was just him.

Fuck. Was he flirting with her?

Aye. That he was.

And he had not an inkling as to her identity. She could be anyone. A lady, a mistress. *Hell*, she could be a duchess. Not too goddamn likely, but the possibility remained.

"Hazard may appeal to some. Not to me, however," she said.

"Finding a man to bed you does?" he asked, then cursed himself for the looseness of his tongue.

Gen would bludgeon him with the nearest available object for this, if she were to ever hear of it.

Number one hundred four pursed her lips. "You are being dismissive."

"Fancy words. All I do is run a gaming house."

"You are suggesting I should not wish for a lover," she elaborated, surprising him with her bravado.

The word *lover*, spoken in her dulcet tones, was making his cock hard. Her voice wasn't the only part of her having that particular, unwanted effect upon him, however.

He shook himself from the spell she'd cast upon him. "Men like me don't *suggest*. We say what we mean, and what I'm telling you is that Lady Fortune does not provide the kind of *circumspection* you're after."

"I understand." Her voice was cool, her demeanor icy. "Forgive me for my mistake."

She turned to go once more.

For some reason, a reason that emerged from deep inside him, murky and indistinct and yet forceful, he did not want her to go just yet.

"My lady."

She looked back to him.

"Mayhap I can be of help to you."

* * *

MIRABEL WAS SWIMMING IN SHAME.

Why, oh *why*, had she listened to her sister when Octavia suggested the owner of Lady Fortune could discreetly help her to find a lover?

You'll be wearing your mask, Octavia had said.

Your anonymity is assured there, Octavia had said.

It is better than going to a disreputable house where you can choose a cicisbeo as if you are choosing the color of your evening gown, Octavia had said.

At which point Mirabel had demanded to know how her unwed sister was aware of such houses of ill repute. Octavia had shrugged, offering nothing.

But what neither Octavia nor Mirabel had considered was just how devastatingly handsome the owner of Lady Fortune was. He possessed the sort of masculine beauty that robbed one's breath. That made one's heart leap. That made one's tongue feel as if it had been stitched to the roof of one's mouth.

She could go on, but he had just told her that mayhap he could be of help to her. She was humiliated enough to linger, despite the dreadful manner in which the interview had thus far unfolded. Partially because she wished the floors would open and swallow her whole.

"Your help is no longer required," she managed to say,

sounding like the woman her marriage had forced her to become.

The Duchess of Stanhope was a cold, emotionless, rigid apostle of propriety. At least, she had been, when she'd had no other option. And she still was, according to all who knew her. The social circles in which she traveled were impeccable. Nary a hint of scandal had ever tainted her name.

And that was why, now that Stanhope was gone and her period of mourning was at an end, a secret membership in Lady Fortune and the chance to experience everything she had missed had been decidedly, deliciously appealing. Appealing enough to risk everything for this meeting. There was some comfort in her anonymity, but the social damage which could befall her children should word of her indiscretion spread remained a terrifying danger.

He stepped nearer to her, bringing with him the scent of citrus and leather. And bringing his impossible magnetism as well. The man was a walking, breathing invitation to sin, from the tousled mahogany waves of his hair to those dark, spellbinding eyes, to the fall of his cravat. And that was to say nothing of his height, his broad shoulders, long legs...

Lady Fortune's owner raised an ungloved finger and dared to touch her, tracing the bare patch of skin beneath the gold-and-ruby necklace adorning her throat. That rough pad swept along her collarbone, sending a trail of answering fire burning straight through her.

"Are you certain it is no longer required, my lady?" he pressed. "You are lingering."

Any woman would have tarried with this man, just to remain in his presence for another minute. But she did not say that, for it would be more foolish than all the revelations she had thus far made.

"I am certain. Once again, I beg your pardon."

His finger was still upon her, tracing slowly, *branding*. "I could be your lover."

His words shocked her. Someone gasped, and she knew it must have been her, yet she had no recollection of forming the sound, so thoroughly had he taken her by surprise. "You?"

He considered her, that maddening forefinger hovering on her hungry skin.

When was the last time she had been touched by a man for the sake of touching alone? She could not recall. Stanhope had bedded her out of necessity, and after she had given him an heir and a spare—three children later—he had never again visited her bed. His defection had been a relief rather than a disappointment, but now, she longed for connection.

For *this*.

With this man.

"Me," he said.

Her every sense came alive.

"I…"

"Need a lover," he finished for her, smiling slowly.

With wicked intent.

She felt that smile in the ache that blossomed to life between her thighs. "Need seems a bit strong of a word."

"Require seems just as strong, no?"

He was not wrong, and yes, that was how she had initially phrased her request. Had it been an ill-chosen word? Her head was muddled. Her tongue, tangled. Her body, aflame.

"You are offering yourself?" she asked.

His lips twitched, as if he found the situation—mayhap Mirabel—amusing. "Aye. Myself."

What was she thinking? This man would never do for what she wanted. He was too strong. Too virile. Too handsome. Too…*everything*.

She shook her head. "No."

His brows rose. "Why not, madam?"

"You are too young," she said. "You look to be no more than five-and-twenty."

"Eight-and-twenty," he countered.

Ten years her junior and a rake by the look of him, she had no doubt.

"Near enough," she said dismissively. "Thank you for the offer, sir, but I must decline. I would also beg you to keep this matter between the two of us."

But still, he had not released her. Instead, his fingers circled the back of her neck, cupping her in a manner that was possessive and yet gentle.

"Why must you? Decline, that is?"

Why indeed? His head had dipped toward hers, bringing their mouths perilously close. And she was once more ensnared. Physically, she could escape him with ease, she knew. He was not holding her tightly, nor forcing her in any fashion. The trouble was, she had no wish to flee. She was complicit. Every wicked urge she possessed was exhorting her to stay where she was.

"I was given to understand that clubs for gentlemen offered companionship of a certain nature for their patrons. I assumed Lady Fortune to operate in the same manner for its female members. But this…you…I cannot."

"I assure you that you can." His gaze searched hers.

"I do not know your name." Her voice was breathless, and her protest was a blatant attempt at removing herself from this man's intoxicating presence.

"Demon Winter." He smiled.

Everything inside her turned to liquid.

What a name.

The personification of everything dangerous and forbidden.

"Demon?"

His lips drew nearer, almost grazing hers. "Aye. 'Tis me."

"You do not know my name." After this bit of nonsense emerged from her, she wished she could rescind the words. What foolishness. Of course this man did not know her name. Nor would she wish him to. That was the beauty of Lady Fortune—anonymity. And that was what she required, complete and utter discretion.

"Do you *want* me to know it, *number one hundred four?*" he asked.

What would be the harm, she reasoned, in the revelation of just her given name, nothing more?

"No," she blurted, out of her depths and unprepared for this meeting in more ways than she had ever anticipated. "The less you know of me, the better."

"Or the more of you I know, the better," he suggested.

She liked his deep baritone. It washed over her like a caress. There was nothing polished or polite or aristocratic about this man. He was bold and roguish and rugged. A different kind of longing speared through her.

Wrong, cautioned the voice within, the one which had rigidly ruled her life for the last fifteen years. The one which sounded a great deal like Stanhope's.

This is wrong.

She had been tempted to reveal her given name. Had allowed him to touch her. What had she been thinking?

All the weight of her marriage came tumbling down upon her at once, crushing. Mirabel jerked away from Demon Winter and the temptation he presented, severing the contact although she regretted it.

"I cannot..." She tried to find an explanation that would suffice and failed. "I must go."

Before the last word fled from her lips, she had already turned to flee.

CHAPTER 2

"You *do* realize you cannot remain in hiding all day, do you not?"

Mirabel frowned at Octavia over her chocolate cup's gold-edged rim. The ducal crest was carefully facing out; the less Mirabel saw of it, the better. Unfortunately, she still knew it was there, likely mocking her poor sister. Octavia had never liked Stanhope any more than Mirabel had.

But never mind that. Most people hadn't been fond of the Duke of Stanhope, with the dubious exception of his mistresses.

"Of course I can remain abed all day," she told her sister. "I shall feign an ailment and no one will know the difference. It will be just as it was whenever Stanhope was in residence."

Toward the end of their marriage, before her husband's death, the duke had been in residence on a sole occasion per year—enough to see his heirs and ignore Joanna, their middle child. Then, he would return to the home he kept for his mistress, where he preferred to stay. Mirabel had been glad for his absence, but she had remained his prisoner just the same. The Duke of Stanhope could bed every lightskirt in town, whilst Mirabel was expected to remain a paragon of virtue.

Or face her husband's wrath.

The reminder sent a shiver down her spine, but she chased away the memories of those long-ago days, for Stanhope could no longer hurt her now. He could haunt the past all he wished, but there was no place for him in the present, where she and Octavia were comfortably ensconced in the sitting area of Mirabel's bedchamber.

Unfortunately, by the harsh light of morning, her shame and guilt over her behavior at Lady Fortune the previous evening threatened to overwhelm.

"The children would fret over you, and you know it," Octavia countered in fond tones.

She was an indulgent aunt. Octavia loved Percy, Joanna, and Gideon as if they were her own. And Octavia was right—Mirabel's beloved children would wonder at her extended absence. They were the only good which had come of her miserable match with Stanhope.

Well, her children and her newfound freedom, tentative though it was. But the latter had emerged from the end of her marriage instead.

"I expect my darlings would," she acknowledged. "However, this morning, I needed some privacy in which to hang my head in shame. I feel like a fool. Why did you allow me to believe the owner of Lady Fortune would be able to assist me in my effort to find a...my *endeavor?*"

She could not bear to utter the word *lover* now. Not when the mere thought of it brought with it more heat than embarrassment. More thoughts of *him*. Demon Winter. Even his name was a sin.

Octavia shrugged, looking blithe. "Because I thought they would. Everyone who has ever seen a print shop caricature knows gaming hells are filled with bawds. Why should one suppose a gaming hell for ladies is any different? Moreover, the anonymity you have there seemed the perfect foil for seeking a lover without inviting scandal, and I know how much care you take with your reputation."

Mirabel almost choked on her chocolate. "Do you mean to tell me you based your authority in the matter upon *caricatures*?"

The scandal-mongering print shops in London were notorious for their scathing depictions of society. She knew Octavia sent servants to obtain them frequently; as the lady of the house, it was impossible not to. However, she had not supposed her sister's recommendation had been solely based upon the lewd scribblings of caricaturists.

Why had she listened to Octavia? Should she not have known better by now? Her sister was forever getting into scrapes. Her lack of adherence to societal demands was what had rendered her unweddable. At least, according to polite society. And their mother.

Octavia had the grace to look a bit shamefaced. "Pray do not be vexed with me. The caricatures have never been wrong before."

Mirabel frowned, for she refused to view such nonsense. In the early years of her marriage, she had been featured in them with a frequency that had been most distressing, but Octavia had likely been unable to get her hands upon them then, ruled as she had been by their proper mother. "Surely they have had occasion to be wrong."

Her sister schooled her features into a look of feigned innocence. "Not once."

"You are an incorrigible hoyden." Mirabel said the last without rancor, for it was impossible to be angry with her sister. Octavia was sweet, kind, outspoken, and eccentric, and she was blessed with a generous heart. A combination which promised to see her spirits crushed and her heart broken in any society marriage.

"I am a spinster," Octavia corrected her. "An incorrigible *spinster*, if you please. I shall own my faults, and my age is among them. You are saving me from my fate as a companion to some dreadful dowager and her dogs, and I shall be forever grateful. The least I can do is to help you to find a man to—"

"Enough, my dear," Mirabel interrupted primly, her cheeks going hot. "If your age is a detriment, I shudder to think what mine is."

Octavia was nearly ten years her junior. So was Mr. Demon Winter.

And he was devilishly handsome as well.

Too young, she chided herself. *Too wrong for the task.* If indeed there could be a task. She was woefully inept at the business of being a wicked widow in secret, having never experienced wickedness herself. Stanhope's visit to her bed had been perfunctory at best and painful at worst.

"Do cease pretending you are ancient," her sister said. "We both know you are not, just as we both know you promised to tell me what happened at Lady Fortune in great detail. I am waiting."

"I have already told you more than enough." She took a sip of her chocolate in an attempt to calm her rapidly beating heart. "I requested a meeting, asked for assistance, and was informed I was incorrect in my assumption."

Such a bland way to describe what had happened in the private room. As if the scorching, deliciously tempting Mr. Demon Winter had never inhabited the same chamber as she had at all. As if he had not touched her and set her aflame. One day later, and she still knew the brand of his touch. It lingered on her skin, burning with sweet, suppressed pleasure, a call to arms she had to ignore.

"Yes, but that scarcely tells me anything at all." Octavia scooted to the edge of her chair, eyes wide with anticipation. "What did he look like, this Mr. Winter?"

Diabolically handsome.

"He was uninteresting." She drained the rest of her chocolate in one unladylike gulp to keep from saying anything else.

"Your countenance does not suggest he was uninteresting."

Sisters. Specifically, *this* one.

She skewered Octavia with a pointed glare. "You have caused me enough trouble for now. Let us leave this story as it is."

"He is handsome, is he not?"

Her cheeks were on fire. So, too, the tips of her ears. "No."

"He is!" Octavia chortled. "Oh, Mirabel, you have never been capable of telling a falsehood."

And what a pity that was. An affinity for lying would have served her well in her marriage. Lord knew it had been a boon for Stanhope.

"Mr. Winter was fine enough looking, I suppose," she allowed, consternated by the continued heat in her cheeks, and by the steady pulse of desire, deep within. A part of her she had not known existed was blossoming to life. All because of one man. "If one is attracted to the dangerous, rough-hewn, lowborn sort."

"Oh dear."

Mirabel frowned at her sister. "What is the matter?"

"Once again, your countenance, dear sister. You give yourself away, I fear."

She was sure she did not. She was completely, utterly certain there was no means by which Octavia could possibly know how hopelessly attracted she had been to Mr. Demon Winter. How that sinful man had made her heart beat fast. How he had planted the seed of desire deep within her. And how hastily that seed had burst open, curling upward, reaching, growing, searching for the light.

Or, in this case, the darkness that surely was Mr. Winter.

"Nonsense," she clipped, both to her wildly meandering thoughts and to Octavia.

"Dangerous, rough-hewn, and lowborn, you say?" her sister repeated with a smirk.

Mirabel tried to take another sip of her chocolate, only to belatedly realize she had already emptied her cup. How embarrassing. It would seem she had no pride today.

She settled the cup on its saucer and waved a dismissive hand. "Altogether unacceptable. Not at all the sort of man whom one should know."

"Hmm," was all Octavia said, pausing before her brows furrowed. "Where is Grandmother's ruby ring? I do not believe I have seen your finger without it."

Mirabel froze, staring at her hand which was, indeed, bereft of all ornamentation. It would not have been strange at this time of the morning, when she was in dishabille in her private apartments except for one fact. She had not removed the ring, which was a treasured reminder of the woman she still missed, more like a mother to them than their own mother had been.

Her heart pounded with a different sort of insistence now.

Grandmother's ring was gone.

"I do not know where it can be," she said, her chest growing suddenly tight as she struggled to think of where she may have left or lost it.

"Think," Octavia urged her softly. "Were you wearing it when you attended Lady Fortune last evening?"

She had been. Mirabel recalled fidgeting with it as she awaited Mr. Winter in the private room, and as a crushing sense of panic had descended upon her. Little different than the anxiety assailing her now, in fact. She was selfish to seek her pleasure when one wrong move could prove so incredibly ruinous for herself, for Octavia, for her children.

"I was wearing it yesterday." She paused, traveling through the evening in her mind. "There was a moment, when a lad was aiding me with my wrap and gloves... I was in such a rush to flee, I fairly ran from Lady Fortune."

She had thrown on her wrap, then bundled herself into her waiting carriage, still a tangled knot of emotion and embarrassment. The lad had been grinning. Standing nearer to her than she was accustomed. None of her servants had ever encroached upon her, and in her discomfiture, she had supposed it had been down to his youth and lack of experience. But now...

"Do you suppose he was a pickpocket?" her sister asked, before Mirabel could complete the thought within her mind.

"I do not know." She squared her shoulders. "All I *do* know is that I am going to have to return to Lady Fortune."

"Splendid," Octavia pronounced.

"Not splendid." A grim sense of portent filled her. "Not splendid at all."

FOR THE SECOND evening in a row, Demon found himself ensconced in a private room with *number one hundred four*. On this occasion, however, they were not alone. Instead, they were accompanied by Davy, the sometime pickpocket his brother Dom had taken under his wing. When Gen had opened Lady Fortune, she had inherited Davy. And now that Gen was a married woman, dividing her time between being the wife of a marquess and the hell's secret owner, troublesome young Davy had been bequeathed upon Demon.

Last night, following *number one hundred four's* abrupt

flight from this chamber, Davy had helped her into her wrap. Whilst doing so, he had apparently helped her *out* of a valuable gold and ruby ring. Now, Demon was tasked with making amends to the lady in question and hoping to hell she wouldn't run about the tables informing every masked lady in attendance there was a pickpocket in their midst.

The little shite was going to get a tongue lashing from Gen, and that would be after Demon made certain he was returned to chamber pot removal duties as penance for thievery. The scamp loved filching. No doubt, it was in his blood. But fleecing fine ladies at Gen's hell was akin to a bird with a broken wing. It wasn't going to fly.

"I understand you have something of mine in your possession," said *number one hundred four*.

And here was the part that made Demon itchy. Which was damned odd. He'd never felt a hint of guilt at past deceptions. How bloody lovely for it to happen now, before the woman he'd scared off the night before. It had been the first time in his life that offering to bed a woman had sent her running in the opposite direction.

"Aye," Demon forced himself to say, knowing it was in the best interest of Lady Fortune yet still feeling like an arse for what he was about to do. "There is a reason I invited the lad here to our meeting, my lady. After I received your message concerning the ring, I went directly to everyone here, didn't I, Davy?"

Davy tucked his head, nodding. "Aye, Mr. Winter. That you did."

"We all agreed we must search the hell for your ring," Demon carried on smoothly, hating himself for the impending lie. "Our search turned up naught."

"Naught?" *Number one hundred four* was frigid, unyielding. "You claimed to have my ring. Sir, if you have brought me here for no reason, I will be most displeased."

She had the airs of a duchess, this one.

He flashed her a smile. "Patience, my lady. Davy is a right hero. He had the notion to search for your ring in this room, and this is where it was found. Give it up to the lady, lad."

He nudged young Davy betwixt the bony shoulder blades.

Davy moved forward dutifully, holding the ring out for her ladyship.

She took it, inspecting it hastily before nodding. "Thank you, Master Davy. I appreciate your dedication, and I cannot convey how happy I am to have the ring back in my possession."

Demon was relieved the bauble was indeed hers. One never knew with the young rascal; Davy likely had a horde of stolen jewels hidden somewhere. But Demon also found himself curious about the ring and its importance to the lady. It was a simple enough gold band, ornamented with a ruby. Hardly equal to the value she had placed upon it, storming into Lady Fortune this evening and demanding a reckoning.

Her sudden appearance had taken him by surprise. After the manner in which she had fled the night before, he had not expected her to reappear.

Davy bowed, the scamp. "Happy I found it for you, my lady."

"That will be all, lad," Demon told Davy firmly. "Return to your post."

"The bleedin' chamber pots? But I ain't—"

"You are in the presence of a lady," Demon reminded the lad. *And one you have recently thieved.*

"Pardon," Davy said, hanging his head again and shuffling his feet as he tugged at his forelock. "Never intended to pay insult."

Number one hundred four slid the ring back on her finger before lowering herself to Davy's height. She settled her hands on his thin shoulders. "My dear sir, pray do not tell me you are being asked to perform a task so unpleasant?"

Davy cast a sly glance in Demon's direction before turning his attention back to the lady whose compassion was likely to make her a mark for a second thieving of that cursed ring. Demon settled his eye upon it, praying Davy would not make another attempt.

"Mr. Winter tells me I 'ave to clean up the piss pots," Davy confided in *number one hundred four*. "Says he'll box my ears if I don't."

The cursed little shite. He blinked in exaggerated fashion, as if he were attempting to keep tears at bay. Naturally, he said nothing of the reason for his duty. Demon had never once threatened Davy with punishment other than the performing of unpleasant tasks, and that had only been made necessary by the lad's continued purloining from their patron's reticules, fingers, necks, and whatnot. He had no choice but to watch as Davy wrapped the lady around his thieving pinky finger.

Demon bit his lip to keep from uttering a vicious oath.

"Oh my darling boy," she murmured, her tone properly horrified. "Do not cry, I beg you."

She held the boy to her in a motherly embrace. Demon winced as he saw Davy's fingers creeping perilously near to the lady's earbobs. He quickly tapped the back of the lad's shoe with his boot, warning him he was being watched. Davy's hand moved away.

The lad gave an exaggerated sniffle, as if he withheld a sob.

"That is quite enough, lad," Demon warned grimly.

Davy was going to get a tongue lashing from *him* after this display. Never mind Gen. It wouldn't wait that long.

The lady rose to her full height, her blue eyes finding Demon. "Mr. Winter, this is egregious treatment of young

Master Davy, and especially after he was responsible for finding my ring. I insist you reward him rather than offering punishment."

"Doing his duties isn't punishment," Demon groused, shooting the lad a pointed glare to let him know this would not go unavenged. "He gets his wages."

He was going to hang the lad by his damned thumbs, that was what he was going to do.

"He deserves to be absolved of his duties for at least a week after his recovery of my ring. It belonged to my grandmother, and it is quite priceless to me."

Christ. This was all going the wrong bloody way. Demon flicked a glance in the lady's direction once more, wondering if she was serious. The half of her countenance visible beneath her mask was unsmiling. The sooner this farce was over, and the sooner this maddening woman was gone, the better.

"He will be absolved," Demon said through gritted teeth.

I'll absolve the thieving little bastard with chamber pot duty for the next damned century.

"I require your word," she pressed.

His word? *Ha!*

He smiled, though it was damned painful to do so. "You have it, my lady."

That was not a lie, not entirely. He could play her game.

She nodded, regal as any queen. "Thank you, sir."

He bit his tongue, then pinned Davy with a narrow-eyed glare which promised later retribution. "Go now, lad."

Davy gave his forelock another tug and disappeared from the room.

At last.

Demon suppressed a sigh as he turned back to *number one hundred four.*

"It would seem you have a pickpocket on your hands, Mr. Winter," she said, taking him utterly by surprise.

But he wasn't one of the best bleeding gamblers in the East End for nothing.

He eyed her calmly. "Rest assured, I would know if we did, my lady."

She pursed her lips, and damn if that did not make him long to kiss them.

"I believe you *do* know, Mr. Winter. Do not, I beg you, dare to ply me with your charm. It shall not work."

"Believe me, my lady, if I were plying you with charm, you would know it," he said, keeping his voice low. Intimate.

There were other ways he would like her to beg him. Delicious ways. *Floating hell*, why was he suddenly thinking of this delectable, aristocratic lady in his bed, his to sweetly torment? What was it about her ice which turned him to flame?

Demon cocked his head, considering her. This evening, she wore a gauze and satin gown in a shade of ivory that complemented the fiery curls framing her face. French kid gloves to her elbows, a fringe of lilac silk flowers adorning the hem of her gown, her delicate slippers peeping from beneath. She was the perfect blend of proper and forbidden, and he wanted to debauch her. Thoroughly.

He wanted her in his bed wearing nothing but her mask.

But alas, he was not going to have his way. She had already refused him, and he would do well to remember that stinging blow to his pride. Trouble was, his pride and his prick weren't speaking much these days. Had they ever been?

"The young gentleman you have tasked with emptying chamber pots is the same one who helped me with my wrap yesterday," she persisted, breaking through Demon's troublesome thoughts. "He thieved my ring as he did so."

Damn it. No more allowing Davy his run of Lady Fortune.

"For a lady who was just singing the lad's praises, you're awfully certain he's a moll-buzzer."

In an effort at distracting her, Demon had intentionally used the flash word for a pickpocket who targeted women.

"Moll-buzzer, Mr. Winter?" She frowned.

And she was deuced pretty with her lush lips turned down. But he oughtn't be noticing that just now. Instead, he pretended he had heard a knock on the door.

"I'll be there in a moment," he called, then returned his voice to its ordinary pitch as he addressed *number one hundred four*. "Was there something else I could assist you with, my lady?"

Her eyes narrowed. "Someone is at the door? I did not hear a knock."

He was going to need a flash of lightning after this—a whole glass of gin straight down his throat. "Aye. I've a club to run, madam. Unless there is something else you need from me? Another request for a lover, perhaps?"

He was taunting her, and he should not have done. But she was riling him in a way he had not experienced before. And he didn't bloody well like it. Mayhap he needed to tell Gen to—

"Yes."

He blinked. Stilled. Surely she was not suggesting she wanted him to find her a lover?

"There is indeed something else I need, Mr. Winter," she said, her voice dripping with frost and disapproval. "I would like to take young Master Davy with me. A lad such as Davy, being forced to empty chamber pots, is an egregious sin. Likely, his wages are so meager he feels he has no choice but to steal from your patrons. You ought to be ashamed."

For a moment, he had no words. And Demon Winter robbed of speech was a rare sight indeed.

Where to begin?

25

Then, another devil entered his thoughts. Why begin at all? Could he not simply allow the lady before him to delude herself into believing Davy was an innocent, given no choice but to thieve from his betters for his bread?

"You want to take him with you, my lady?"

She nodded. "Indeed, I do. He shall be far happier with me, installed at my household, than he is here."

"As a servant?"

"As a *guest*."

Demon's lips twitched. This was too bloody good. If he could not bed this luscious, red-haired siren, then at least he could have himself an excellent laugh over the notion of Davy running wild all over her ladylike abode.

"As you wish."

She smiled then, and fuck him if he did not feel the effect of that smile all the way to his darkened, tarnished, tattered soul. "Excellent."

There were so many things Demon wanted to say, but in the end, he swallowed each one of them down. This was for the best, he told himself. He would be rid of two problems at once. No more pickpocket in the ranks, and no more *number one hundred four* to plague him.

"He may accompany me this night," she added, piercing Demon's thoughts once more. "How old is he, do you suppose?"

"Depends on the lad's mood when you ask," Demon said wryly. "Could be nine. Could be twelve."

His response did nothing to deter the lady, however.

She nodded. "Close enough in age to my eldest son. I will be awaiting young Master Davy in my carriage, Mr. Winter. Do see that he is brought round."

With that, she swept past Demon, quitting the chamber.

And Demon would be lying if he said he did not watch the sway of her hips as she took her leave.

CHAPTER 3

*B*y breakfast the next morning, it had become apparent that Mirabel had misjudged her newest houseguest. In the cheerful gold salon she had always favored, she found herself surrounded by her children, her sister, and one Master Davy. Four voices sounded at once.

"My ruby earbobs are missing."

"I cannot find Father's signet ring."

"My favorite wooden horse is gone."

"Where is my toy theater?"

Her children and Octavia were not alone in their sudden losses. Mirabel's silver hairbrush had also disappeared.

There was only one reasonable suspect. And she had brought him to Tarlington House the evening before in what she could now acknowledge had perhaps been a mistake.

"Davy," she said slowly, addressing the adorable towheaded lad. "Have *you* anything missing?"

He grinned, showing a missing tooth. "Just me front cog."

Dear God. Was cog another word for tooth?

Mirabel sighed. "Do you recall the discussion we had on the carriage ride here last evening, Master Davy?"

"Aye."

Patience, Mirabel. Have patience for this lad, who has neither mother nor father in his life.

"And what was the discussion?" she prodded gently.

"I'm to follow your rules, My Grace."

"*Your* Grace," Mirabel reminded.

"My Grace?" His brow wrinkled and he appeared endearingly befuddled, even if he was a perpetual thief. "I ain't got none."

She suppressed a sigh. The child was quick-witted—that much was apparent. She did not know if he was feigning confusion to fluster her or if he was in earnest. But she would have to settle for the latter.

"I am a duchess, Davy," she pressed on. "To address me with the proper respect, you must call me *Your* Grace not *My* Grace."

Davy scratched his head, leaving a hank of hair comically askew. "Confusing is what all this fancy shite is. I were happy at Lady Fortune, ma'am. That I were. You can take me back. I promise I'll never bite your ring again."

Bite her ring? *Good heavens*, where to begin?

Before she could formulate a proper response, the voices of her children and Octavia rose once more, creating a cacophony that was sufficient to give anyone a blistering case of the megrims.

"Never say you found the source of your missing ring and decided to bring him here so that he may linger beneath this roof and rob us further," her sister drawled.

"Why is he here?" demanded Percy.

"I want my horse!" shouted Gideon.

"I shall never be able to play toy theater again!"

The last was issued by Joanna, who enacted a dramatic pose and pressed the back of her hand to her forehead. The girl possessed the theatrics of an actress.

Mirabel ought to have presided over the morning introductions and Mirabel knew it. However, when she had returned to Tarlington House bearing an unanticipated guest, her children had already been abed. She had seen to it that the governess, Walters, had been made aware of the new arrival and seen him settled. Afterward, Mirabel had spent the remainder of the night in fitful tossing and turning in her bed, unable to sleep, thanks to one man.

But she would not think of Demon Winter now.

No, indeed. She would not think about his sensual smile or his deep voice or his intoxicating scent. Nor would she recall the way he made her feel whenever they were in proximity. *Alive.* And aflame.

So hopelessly, desperately, aflame.

She tamped down the unwanted longing. "Davy is our guest. We will treat him with the respect which he is due. However, Master Davy, you must be mindful of the rules in this household. No vulgar language and no thieving. You will address me as Your Grace. You shall call the rest of our assemblage as they are named: Stanhope, Lord Gideon, Lady Joanna, and Lady Octavia."

"If you return my ruby earbobs, I shall allow you to call me Auntie Octavia as these other scamps do," Octavia informed Davy with a wink.

"What if I don't got 'em?" he asked.

Octavia's eyes narrowed. "You and I both know you have them, you little rogue."

Davy shrugged, then crossed his arms over his bony chest, his expression turning mulish. "Take me back to Lady Fortune."

It occurred to Mirabel, quite for the first time, that Davy may not view her rescue of him as a boon. Rather, he may consider it quite the opposite. Before her was evidence of the difference in social strata for her children and this lad. He was clad in the clothing he had been wearing the evening before, though she had directed Walters to provide him with some of Percy's garments. His hair was ill-cut, his speech was improper, and yet he was nearly of an age with her eldest son. Percy was already a duke, and Davy did not know the proper means of addressing a duchess.

"Do you wish to return to Lady Fortune?" she asked him softly, wondering if she had done more harm than good for him in bringing him to her home.

"Aye." He tugged at his forelock, looking agitated. "I likes it there, My Grace."

"Your Grace," she tried again.

He scowled. "I already told you, I haven't none."

"You are mussing it up," Joanna offered. "You must call Mama *Your Grace*, and you must say *I have not any*, not *I haven't none*."

Davy flicked a dismissive glance in Joanna's direction. "You're scarcely older than a babe. I'll not be 'eeding the likes of you."

Joanna sniffed. "I want my theater."

"What makes you think I've got it, My Grace?" he asked Joanna.

Mirabel's daughter sighed, giving her golden curls a shake. "He is a hopeless cause, Mama."

"Not as hopeless as he would have us believe," Mirabel observed.

The lad had an elaborate act. That much was apparent. She could not discern how much of it was real and how much exaggerated for effect. She could not be certain he was thieving because it was a ruse or because he liked the attention he received when he was caught. Mayhap the lad could not help himself.

Either way, he had proven himself untrustworthy after just one night beneath her roof. He wanted to return to Lady

Fortune. She was willing to give him his wish, with one condition.

Unfortunately, that condition meant she would need to face Mr. Demon Winter one more time.

"Lad," she said softly, sinking to her knees before him. "If you want to be at Lady Fortune, I will be happy to return you. The reason I brought you here is because of the ill treatment you reported receiving there."

Davy's cheeks went ruddy, and he hung his head. "Aye, well, that…it weren't as bad as what I said."

"Wasn't," she corrected gently. "Were you thieving because you required the funds, Master Davy, or were you doing it because you enjoyed the thrill?"

He kicked at the Aubusson, still refusing to meet her gaze. "I didn't need the blunt."

But Mirabel had to be certain. "And Mr. Winter, he is fair to you?"

"It's a square deal I got there. I shouldn't 'ave filched your ring, My Grace. I'm sorry for it. Didn't mean to cause you no troubles."

"*Your* Grace," Joanna offered helpfully.

"And all the items which are currently missing in the household?" Mirabel persisted, not bothering to correct the lad.

"I'll see it's returned." He kicked at the carpets some more. "And I'll fetch the silver, the teacup, the shiner, the ink well, the book…"

"Oh dear," Mirabel whispered to herself as the lad droned on with the list of his ill-gotten gains.

"Oh dear indeed," her sister said, raising a dark brow. "You must send him back from whence he came."

Yes, she must.

Drat it all.

And drat Demon Winter the most.

***

FOR THE THIRD night in a row, Demon found himself ensconced in a private room with *number one hundred four*.

She had returned, wearing a gown that appeared as if it had been fashioned of a cloud.

And her eyes were spitting fire.

The evening had just gotten a hell of a lot more interesting.

He grinned. "My lady."

Christ, she was beautiful, and he wanted to strip her naked and lay claim to every luscious part of her with his tongue first and his cock second. He wanted to fall to his knees, lift her skirts, and suck on her pearl until her legs went weak and she screamed his name.

The violence of his lust had to be tamed.

She is someone's mother, he tried to remind himself. When she had offered to take Davy on last night—hell, when she had *demanded* it—he had not missed the reference to her son. He had to admit, he may well have swived women who were mothers before. But since they had never mentioned their children, he had also never asked. Had never considered the notion. It seemed impossible to believe the ethereal, alluring beauty before him was old enough to be mother to a lad near in age to Davy.

The urge to see her without her mask had become an itch he could not scratch. Must not scratch. Wanted to scratch very, very badly.

"Mr. Winter," she clipped, voice dipped in ice.

His cock went rigid.

"To what do I owe the privilege of this evening's visit?" he asked, feeling impish. "In search of more orphans you can snatch away? Mayhap you've misplaced another bauble and you need someone to blame?"

Her lips tightened. "Of course not, sir."

He liked the way she called him *sir*. Liked everything about her far, far too much, in fact. This woman could land him in a dilemma, and Demon knew it. A delicious, wrong, seductive dilemma.

He moved nearer, drawn to her sophisticated grace, to the lovely elegance of her. She was a combination of prudish and tempting that he could not seem to resist.

"No?" He stroked his jaw, allowing his gaze to rake over her feminine form as he considered her. "Have you returned because you have decided to reconsider my offer? If so, madam, I must warn you, it's no longer available."

That was a lie.

But if there was one thing Demon Winter excelled at, it was playing games. Whether dice, cards, or women, he knew how to wager, and he knew how to win. And this fiery-haired beauty was going to be his. He had just decided it. To hell with all the reasons why he should not have her.

"Of course I have not," she said, her tone just as frigid as before.

But there was an undercurrent there, an awareness. He did not miss it. Her eyes dipped to his mouth fleetingly.

"Are you certain, my lady?" He stopped before her, near enough to touch.

Near enough, her exotic scent invaded his senses.

Her lips parted, her tongue gliding over them. "You are a scoundrel to remind me of my folly."

He grinned. "Not a scoundrel, love. A scoundrel would have taken what you offered three nights ago."

She inhaled sharply. "Mr. Winter, you are insolent."

"You like it," he dared.

And he did not think he was wrong about this, about the connection sparking between them, like flint ready to produce a flame.

"I..." She paused, faltering.

He had flustered her. Her throat had gone pink. So too, the tops of her breasts. That was when he noted the smattering of freckles on her skin. Charming little flecks adorning her like gems, more noticeable given the flush spreading over her.

"You were saying," he prompted, tempted to trace the pattern. Somehow, he maintained his restraint.

"I came to return Davy," she said suddenly.

Disappointing change of subject, that. Demon did not want to think of the lad, not when desire was hanging hot and heavy in the air. Not when he was about to touch her. Kiss her. Pleasure her.

Damn.

"That did not last long." His observation was laced with humor, for he had expected Davy's swift return.

"You know he is a thief," she charged.

He inclined his head. "Aye. The lad has quick fingers."

"You knew he stole my ring."

Guilty.

"I suspected it." As they exchanged words, she began a slow retreat. And he followed. Step by step. Until she backed into the wall. He braced his palms on the plaster beside her head. "No one asked you to take the scamp under your wing, as I recall. That was all your idea."

"I thought you were mistreating him." The ice had melted from her voice.

He shook his head. "I ain't in the business of abusing children, madam. Davy is part of the family here, and we are doing our best to keep him from thieving."

"Yet you allowed me to take him."

"Aye. Because I knew he'd be back."

She said nothing, simply stared.

Mother of all saints, her eyes were not just blue. They were gray too, with hints of violet, and her lashes were long and coppery beneath that cursed mask.

"Nothing to say, *number one hundred four?*" he taunted.

"Mirabel."

Demon leaned nearer. "Begging your pardon?"

Out came that tongue again, wetting her lips, making him mad. "My name. It is Mirabel."

"Mira." He tried the name, liking the way it sounded, the way it felt, the intimacy humming between them.

"Mirabel," she corrected primly.

"Mira," he said again, enjoying their verbal swordplay.

They hovered on the edge of something more.

Something wondrous.

"You are a stubborn man, Mr. Winter."

He nodded. "I'll not deny it. You may call me Demon if you like."

"You do not look like a demon," she said softly. "'Tis far too harsh a name for a man as…"

Once more, her words trailed off. But he wanted them. Wanted them as much as he wanted her.

"A man as…" he prodded.

"A man as beautiful as you," she whispered.

Victory.

The surge of desire within him was potent and instant.

"Damian," he found himself telling her.

Why, he could not say. He had not used his given name since he'd been a lad of Davy's age.

"Damian," she repeated.

Christ, his name in her voice. It was a thing of beauty. Mesmerizing.

He was about to break a rule, and he did not give a damn.

Demon tugged lightly at her silken mask. "I want to see your face."

She stilled.

For a moment, he feared she would deny him. Until she reached up, her gloved fingers plucking at the knot holding her mask in place. She whisked the scrap of silk away, casting it to the floor. He reeled at what she revealed.

She was more gorgeous than he had imagined. Bright, wide eyes, high cheekbones, heart-shaped face, full, pink mouth, dainty nose with freckles dancing down the bridge. She stole his breath.

He felt the force of his attraction to her all the way down his body, in his bloody knees.

"Kiss me, Damian."

He could do nothing but obey.

* * *

Her first true kiss, and she had chosen this man.

Damian Winter, gorgeous sinner, altogether unsuitable, brazen and charming and everything she should not want. She had told him her name. Had removed her mask. Had asked him to kiss her. How odd, she thought as his lips moved masterfully over hers that such a tepid, monosyllabic word should be used to describe such incredible, aching fulfillment.

It seemed the center of her body was suddenly her mouth and all the places where they touched. His lips on hers, his hands cupping her face, her palms on his broad chest, a wall of muscled strength. Oh, he was more dangerous than she had supposed.

He had the ability to make her forget everything but him. All the reasons why her anonymity was to remain paramount, the furious desire to maintain her reputation, to protect her children and Octavia, dissipated. She had given him her name, but she wanted to give him far more.

She wanted to give him *everything*.

But for the moment, it was he who was giving. He had claimed her mouth with sudden fervor at first, then slowing and gentling, delivering kisses that were tender and soft. Years of waiting and longing vanished. She had not come here tonight for this, but now that she found herself in his arms, his lips fused with hers, she knew she could not stop. First, he had made his mark upon her name, then her mouth, and now she needed more.

He seemed to understand her lack of experience, for he coaxed her lips with his, guiding her. Her hands crept of their own accord to his shoulders. How she wished she were not wearing gloves. The longing to run her bare fingers through the hair at his nape, to skim her touch over the ridge of his jaw, to absorb his heat, rose within, uncontrollable.

His tongue traced the seam of her mouth, and she was unprepared for the shocking wetness and warmth. She gasped. His tongue slid sinuously against hers. The taste of him flooded her. Sweet, like…chocolate.

How odd it was to think of this bold, powerful man drinking chocolate. She would have supposed he spent his evenings consuming spirits as most gentlemen did. Stanhope had always smelled of brandy and tobacco. But then, there was much about Damian Winter that surprised her.

Tentatively, she moved her tongue against his. The languorous slide made desire settle low in her belly, a new, heavy sense of awareness blossoming between her thighs. He growled and increased the pressure of his mouth on hers, kissing her harder, his tongue delving deeper. Her arms wound around his neck. She pressed herself to him shamelessly, wantonly. Forgetting this was wrong. Forgetting it was forbidden, a terrible idea, far too dangerous…

Her breasts connected with his chest, her already-hard nipples aching. Where he was solid, she was soft. How decadent it was, the crush of her body aligning with his. She had not been prepared for the staggering force of her need. For how much she would want him.

He pulled his mouth from hers, staring down at her with an inscrutable expression. His mahogany hair fell rakishly over his brow. His eyes were dark, twin obsidian discs. His lips were red from the kisses they had shared, his breathing as harsh and ragged as hers. He was so handsome, and she did not regret kissing him though she knew she may later, when she was removed from his intoxicating presence.

For now, it was as if they were the only two people in the building, in London, the world. Just for this charmed span of the next few moments, she could forget everything. Duty, propriety, years of waiting and longing for that which could never be hers...

She felt uncommonly brave beneath his gaze, capable of anything.

"Have you changed your mind, Mira?" he asked softly.

Mira. No one had ever shortened her name but him, and she could not lie, she liked the way it sounded in his gruff baritone.

She struggled to make sense of his words. Her mind was a jumble of his making. Those kisses had robbed her of the ability to speak.

"Why would I have need to change my mind?" she managed past her tingling lips.

Lips that wanted his on them again.

They were still pressed together, her body melting into his.

He rubbed his mouth over hers in the parody of a kiss she desperately desired. Teasing, tempting, luring her under his sensual spell.

"You said you required a lover," he murmured. "Have you found another man?"

Of course she had not. From the instant their gazes had

first connected, Damian Winter had been the only man she wanted. No other would do. Even if it was all wrong. Even if this was dangerous. She recognized that now.

"Are you still offering yourself for the task?" she dared to ask.

"On one condition."

Did she accept?

Yes, said her body.

No, said her inner Duchess of Stanhope.

"What is your condition?" asked her lips, which having a mind of their own, just wanted his upon them once more.

"That I am your only lover. I do not share." He brushed his mouth over hers in the barest whisper of a caress.

Oh.

"I do not share either," she returned.

Which was a lie. She had spent her entire married life sharing her husband with his mistresses. But she had not minded. At least Stanhope had been plaguing them instead of her. The notion of sharing the man before her, however?

Unacceptable, said every part of her.

"While we are lovers, I am yours," he said.

Hers. The notion should not fill her with such a fine frenzy. Should not make her heart pound and her body tingle. Yet, it did. It made her dizzy with desire. Every intention she had possessed in coming to Lady Fortune and meeting with him this evening had disappeared. He was all she wanted.

"Then I am yours as well," she managed past the sudden thickness in her throat.

He kissed her again, and she kissed him back.

When she had been a girl, Mirabel had crawled from a window at Longford Hall, her father's country seat. She had been hiding from a particularly wretched governess, and the roof had seemed a safer alternative to the woman's looming threats of punishment. Until she had gotten on the roof, that was. She recalled how dizzied she had become, staring down at that great height. How perilous her perch.

And that was rather the same way she felt as she kissed this man after promising to become his lover. One wrong step could send her tumbling to her doom. It was thrilling and terrifying in equal measure.

"Come with me," he said against her lips.

He took her hand in his.

And she followed.

CHAPTER 4

*D*emon led Mira through the back halls of Lady Fortune to the private rooms. Although they had formerly belonged to Gen, they were his now that she was a married woman, keeping house in Mayfair. Thank Christ he had seen fit to restore her mask before taking her from the chamber in which they had met this evening. Still, if Gen were to discover he was about to tup one of her patrons…

Why, she would plant him a facer of course.

Like their brother Gav the prizefighter, Gen had a cruel fist.

But never mind that just now, because Mira's fingers were laced with his and she was following him. And he was about to have her where he had been dreaming of her the past few days. In his bed. Against the door. On the floor.

Everywhere he could have her.

As often as possible.

The night was early, and Tiny Tom was on duty. Tiny Tom, so named because he was actually something of a giant, was the man Gen had hired to replace her former right-hand man at Lady Fortune, after the bastard had caused her no end of trouble. Ladies did not get up to nearly as much nonsense as gentlemen did, happily. But that did not mean that either Gen or Demon liked to take chances. Always have a man on duty, and there can be no surprises.

Tonight had been filled with surprises.

But the woman he tugged over the threshold of his private apartments was a different sort of surprise. A good one.

The *best* one.

He closed the door behind them, before taking a moment to drink in the sight of her. That dress like a cloud. That astoundingly lovely hair. Her lips, swollen from his kisses. He still could not believe she was here.

Somehow, they had gone from arguing over Davy and his thieving ways, to kissing, to him bringing her here. And she had come willingly, just as she had kissed him back with an innocent fire which had belied her motherly status. She had kissed him with the inexperience of a maid.

And he found it—and her—utterly intoxicating.

He found the ties of her mask. Gently, he removed it so that he could again study her. The brace of candles which had been lit in anticipation of his return for dinner cast a honeyed glow over her, illuminating the delicacy of her countenance. She was so lovely, he ached. Whilst he had seen many pretty women—and had swived more than his share of them, too—he had never experienced an attraction with greater potency than what he felt for her now.

So strong, his fingers trembled as he traced the smooth skin of her jaw. "You are beautiful, Mira."

Her face was expressive—she was the sort of woman who wore her emotions on her countenance. The mask had been an impediment, but bereft of it, she was on display, easy for him to read. He wondered what he had missed before, when she had been hidden from him.

She looked uncertain now, her expression hesitant. "I am sure you lavish all your conquests with such flattery. You need not use it on me."

She thought herself his conquest? Sweet, innocent Mira. It was *she* who had conquered him. But he was more than happy to keep that secret for now. Forever, if his pride had aught to say about it.

Demon kissed her slowly, softly, showing her with his mouth what he was about to say with his words, before breaking away. "It is not flattery when it is truth. Nor should you be so surprised. Surely you have been told how lovely you are before."

Her lashes fluttered. "Of course I have not."

Her child's father ought to be hanged, drawn, and quartered. The mere thought of the man—of any other man, for that matter—kissing and touching this woman set his teeth on edge. More so, knowing it was a man who did not appreciate her. But then, she had promised Demon he would be her only lover, so at least the bastard was no longer sharing her bed.

"Allow me to make amends." He kissed her again.

She made a delicious sigh of feminine contentment, and twined her arms around his neck. All her ice was turning into fire, and he could not seem to get enough. She was growing bolder. She opened for him without his prompting, her tongue seeking his. It was his turn to groan as a bolt of lust went directly to his prick.

His hands worshiped her curves, following the lines of her waist all the way to her rump, which proved a pleasant handful beneath the fullness of her gown. He cupped her bottom, bringing her nearer until there was nary a space betwixt them. Nothing but yearning, hungry bodies pressed together.

He sucked on her tongue, then nibbled on the succulence

of her lower lip. Christ, the woman was like a sweet confection. He wanted to devour her and treasure her. She was making him mad with her tentative touches and her ravenous kisses. She was one part siren, one part angel, and he had never felt anything like the emotion and need buffeting him.

Demon kissed down her throat, savoring the softness of her skin. Kissing, sucking, hoping he would leave his mark there. Somehow, he found his way to her ear, and when he caught the fleshy lobe in his teeth and tugged, she rewarded him with a throaty moan.

"Tell me what you want, Mira," he murmured, out of his head for her. "Tell me what you need."

"I..." She gasped as he licked the hollow behind her ear. "I do not know what I want...or what I...need."

He raked his teeth along her throat, angling his aching cock against her in an effort to ease some of the relentless need. "Do not be shy, love."

She tensed suddenly in his arms, her fingertips digging into the muscles of his shoulders.

Sensing her turmoil, he raised his head, searching her glittering blue gaze. "Something is wrong."

"It is not shyness which makes me timorous," she blurted, her eyes going wide as if she could not believe what she had just said aloud.

He thought of the hesitance in her kisses, the seeming lack of experience. Confusion hit him.

"You have made love in the past, no? You have a son."

"I do." She nodded, her face going pale. "Perhaps this is a mistake."

Hell no. He was not going to allow her to flee now that he finally had her where he wanted her.

Demon released her bottom and swept a reassuring

caress up her lower back. "You have been intimate with a man before."

She nodded. "I have lain with my husband, but I have never..."

"What you are saying," he began slowly, still grappling with how to make sense of the situation, "is that you have performed the act, but it has never given you pleasure. Is that correct?"

She nodded, looking stricken.

And everything made sense—her request for a lover, her uncertainty.

"Someone ought to throw him off the nearest roof," he growled, thinking of the sacrilege.

A woman as lush and lovely and passionate as Mira, never knowing the heights of desire—it was infuriating. And wrong.

"He is already gone, so there is no need to toss him from a roof," she said quietly.

Ah, a widow. He ought to have recognized it, for he had always held a particular fondness for them. Mira, however, had been lacking in all the familiar traits. She had not been experienced or sure of herself. She had not propositioned him. Instead, she had run after her initial burst of daring.

He wondered how much that daring and her admission just now had cost her.

"Forgive me," he said softly, hoping to avoid spooking her yet again. "It is poorly done to speak ill of the dead."

"Pray, do not speak of him at all. I should not have explained. What must you think of me?"

"I think you are desirable." He kissed her swiftly. "And beautiful." He kissed her again. "And that we will discover together what it is that you like. What it is that you want."

"You...we...will?" She looked adorably dazed.

"Aye." He could make an excellent game of this. Oh hell

yes, he could. "I will try something, and you shall tell me if you like it. And if you truly like it, tell me if you want more."

Mira blinked. "That sounds wicked."

"Everything that's worthwhile is." He grinned, willing her to see the rightness in his suggestion.

Some men took their pleasure and did not give a damn if the women in their bed ever received theirs. Demon Winter was not that sort of arsehole. And he meant to prove it to her, one delicious deed at a time.

"Oh. That could be true. When you say it, I believe it."

Her words struck him. Here was the true Mira, beneath her layers of polish. He had found his way to her.

"Welcome to my wicked world, Mira." He brushed his lips over hers. "Stay as long as you like."

* * *

IF EVER SHE had heard an inducement to debauchery, this was it. The words which had just been uttered by Damian's seductive lips. And the trouble was, she wanted to remain in his wicked world. A part of her wanted to stay forever.

But the practical part of her remained, reminding her she could not. What she *could* do was spend the next few hours here with him. Learning pleasure. Learning herself. Allowing him to do what he would with her.

And had she not already agreed to that when she had entwined her fingers in his and allowed him to lead her here, to his private apartments above Lady Fortune? Of course she had. But she had been so filled with reckless longing that she had not thought about the ramifications until his words had reminded her of just how unskilled she was. Just how unprepared to be this man's lover.

He was gazing down at her now, so earnestly. Awaiting her answer.

"Yes," she whispered.

His grin deepened as he pulled her hands from his shoulders, giving her kid gloves a playful tug. "Let us begin with these. May I?"

He wanted to remove them, she realized, and she wished them gone as well. Mirabel nodded. "Of course."

He surprised her by lifting her right hand to his lips, then catching the tip of her glove's forefinger in his teeth and tugging. The glove slid from her hand. He let it drop to the floor before performing the same ministration to the left glove as well.

She could do nothing but watch as he lifted her fingers to his lips, kissing the knuckles of each one. First her right hand, then her left.

"Do you like this?"

Did he need to ask?

"Yes," she managed.

"Good." He kissed her inner wrist, inhaling as he did so. "I have my answer."

She was flustered. And breathless. All from the attention he had paid her hands, for heaven's sake. "What answer?"

"I wondered whether or not you apply your scent here." He cast her a smile and kissed again. "And you do."

He had wondered? He had noticed her scent?

"Oh," was all she could think to say.

Foolish and silly. She sounded like a hen wit, and she felt like one too.

"Let us discover what else you like, my lady."

"When you called me Mira earlier," she confessed before she could think better of it.

"You liked that?"

She nodded.

"Tell me more about what you like, Mira. What else do

you enjoy?" As he spoke, he was busy. His fingers were working the closures on the back of her gown.

He was disrobing her. And she liked it.

"This."

He peeled her sleeves down her arms, then tugged at her skirts so that her gown fell to the floor, pooling around her slipper-shod feet. She was clad in nothing more than a chemise, her stays, and her stockings.

"What of this?" He took her mouth again.

She could not answer, because his lips were on hers, moving with delicious precision. This man knew how to kiss. At least, she imagined he did, having no comparison.

When he pulled his mouth from hers, she gave him his answer.

"Yes. Oh, yes."

"Good." The smile he gave her warmed her to her toes. "Let us get you out of the rest of your garments and see what else you like."

She had a suspicion it was going to be everything.

Mirabel offered no protest as he stripped her bare. He was a distraction of kisses, caresses, and murmured admiration. Somehow, she was naked and on his bed, and he was still fully clothed as he joined her. She ought to have been embarrassed, but it was as if a delirium of pleasure had settled over her, one of this man's making.

And he was right there with her, his mouth moving over her hungry skin in worshipful kisses, his hands traveling over her in delicious caresses. He kissed a path down her collarbone, to the center of her chest, before dragging his lips lower, between her breasts.

"Do you like this?" he whispered as he kissed her nipple, then blew a stream of hot air over it.

She swallowed. "Yes."

His lips closed over the taut bud, and he sucked.

Glorious sensation blossomed.

He flicked his tongue over her, lapping gently, and the pleasure heightened. She clutched at him, not knowing where to place her hands. Wanting to touch him everywhere. She settled for his coat, frustrated by the layers keeping her from his skin. She attempted to pull it down his shoulders and arms, but he was intent upon lavishing his torture upon first one breast, then the other.

And when he sucked hard, then alternated between raking his teeth over the sensitive flesh and licking, she forgot to care about the fabric keeping her from what she wanted. Because she wanted something else more.

"I like this, too," he told her, sending a smoldering glance in her direction.

He kissed lower then, down her belly, his tongue dipping into the hollow and making her hips buck. His hands were on her thighs, coasting over her and inciting fire everywhere they went. He drew nearer to the center of her, and instead of thinking about duty as she had in the past, all she could think about was how desperately she wanted him there. His lips, his tongue.

Was it possible?

He kissed her mound, then guided her legs wider, opening her to him. His thumb parted her folds and his head dipped. His tongue glided over the bundle of flesh only Mirabel had ever touched.

"Sweet God," she moaned, about to explode into a thousand glittering shards of herself.

"Not God." He sucked, all the while holding her gaze before releasing her with a slow grin. "Just me."

The arrogance of the man.

But on him, it was somehow charming. And he was wonderfully handsome. And his tongue was performing the most incredible feats upon her intimate flesh. She should look away. What he was doing was sinful. Shameful, surely.

He licked down her seam.

His tongue was *inside* her. There. Dear God, *there*.

A sound fled her lips, half moan, half gasp. Her hips jerked up to meet him, bringing him deeper. The wet thrust inside her channel set off ripples of answering desire. She had never experienced anything like it, and as with everything Damian Winter had done to her thus far, she wanted more of it.

More of *him*.

Her fingers sank into his hair, finding purchase in the thick, glossy waves. Without thought, she thrust herself against him, seeking. Searching. He made a low sound of approval and worked his way back to the bud of her sex, where he tortured her with more gentle nips of his teeth and suction.

He slid a finger into her channel. She lost control. Everything within her came undone. The bliss was more intense than anything she had ever experienced, rolling through her like a summer's storm. It was violent, intense, and beautiful. She clenched on his finger and he added a second, stroking deeper as she rode out the wave of her pinnacle.

She lay there, a sated puddle of her former self, her heart pounding, the effervescent glow surrounding her, tangling her thoughts.

He kissed her inner thigh. First one, then the other. "And did you like that, sweet Mira?"

"Oh yes."

* * *

DEMON COULD NOT GET ENOUGH of her.

The delectable woman lying naked in his bed, a flushed

blend of cream and pink, had come beneath his tongue. The memory of the wet clamp of her cunny on his fingers taunted him. His cock ached to be inside her.

But damn it, he was still wearing all his togs. He had been so intent upon giving her pleasure that he had not spared a thought for having to wrest himself from coat, cravat, and trousers whilst sporting a raging pego.

He tore at his coat.

She was so responsive, the last of her ice thoroughly melted. He had done that. He had torn down her walls. Had removed every scrap of her clothing. Had brought her to climax. He still tasted her on his tongue, musk and honey.

His.

Somehow, he could not shake the sense of possession he felt for her. From the moment he had first seen her, all queenly elegance behind her mask, he had felt the inexorable pull.

The same pull he felt now.

This was not going to last, he reminded himself.

They were from different worlds. She was a widow, eager to be touched and to learn passion for the first time. He could give her that knowledge. But that would be all he could give.

"Damian."

His name in her soft, mellifluous voice—the aristocratic accent giving it an edge it had never possessed when his mother had spoken it—shook him from his thoughts. His coat was around his elbows, and he was still wearing his goddamn boots.

"Let me help you," she whispered shyly, rising to a sitting position as she reached for his sleeves.

He allowed her to aid him, ridiculously pleased by the eager way she plucked at his garments. Whoever her husband had been, he had not appreciated the gift he had been given. Demon was glad of it now, for it meant he could be the one to teach her the meaning of pleasure. To discover what her body wanted and needed.

Together, they rid him of his coat, cravat, and waistcoat. He paused to toe off his polished boots. They fell to the floor with two thumps. His shirt was flying over his head and his trousers and stockings were gone as well. They were a tangle of naked limbs. The lush fullness of her breasts against his chest was enough to draw his ballocks tight. As was the sight of her fiery, unbound tresses cascading over his pillow. She was wearing nothing but her jewels, and what an exquisite sight she was to behold.

Mine.

There was that thought again. Wrong, but he would make her his as much as he could before he was through.

Her fingers traced over the inking on his upper arm, the work of Gen, who had painstakingly marked the initials of each bastard Winter sibling there. Soon, he would need to add the rest of his siblings as well, now that they had all become a true family.

"What is this?" Mira asked softly.

"The initials of my brothers and sister," he explained. "We are bound by blood and loyalty, and this is a permanent reminder of that."

The women he had bedded in the past had never asked after the tattoos. It pleased him that Mira cared enough to take note. Her fingers traced the letters slowly, worshipfully.

"It is uniquely beautiful," she murmured.

Ah. If he did not take her soon, he would lose all control. He desired her far, far too much.

"You want this," he said, leveraging himself on one elbow as he cupped her cheek with his free hand.

"I want you," she confirmed.

Need exploded. He was a man beyond control. He settled

between her thighs, his cock pressed to the wet heat of her, and he groaned at how good it felt. How right. How bloody perfect. Then he took her mouth with his. He kissed her long and deep, just the way he intended to fuck her.

The fit of their bodies was natural. He gripped his cock, guiding himself to her entrance. One thrust, and he was inside her. Her legs wrapped around him as her nails bit into his shoulders. Her tongue moved against his and she moaned.

Mother of all saints.

He was in heaven.

Her sheath was tight around him, dripping with the dew of her desire. Slick. So slick. And hot, so hot. He kissed her, staying still until he could not bear it a moment longer and the restless urge to pound into her took over. He withdrew, then slid inside to the hilt once more. Instinct reigned and they moved with a natural rhythm, in unison. Mira arched up to meet him for every thrust.

Their lips fused, tongues mating furiously as their bodies melded. She was nearly there; he could tell by the way she was tightening on him, squeezing his cock so hard, she almost pushed him out. But he was determined. He fucked her harder, deeper, pinning her to the mattress. Taking her with far less finesse than he would have hoped, it was true, but he was too far gone now. She had taken him over the edge.

And he was nothing but lust, desire, passion, and raw, ravaging need.

He wanted her more than he had ever wanted another.

And he wanted her to spend again.

Never breaking their kiss or his stride, he reached between them, finding the swollen nub of her pearl. She was so damn wet and eager, body jerking for more of his touch, a keening cry tearing from her. A sheen of sweat had broken out on his skin, on his brow. Their coupling became carnal and raw.

She reached her crescendo on a strangled scream, her cunny constricting on him as ripples of pleasure rolled through her. Demon was not far from reaching completion himself. Still, he rode out the pleasure for as long as he could. Until he could not bear it. Until he was about to spend inside her. But that would not do. If there was one risk he refused to take, it was siring bastards. He would not visit that same torture upon his own child. He had suffered enough for having been born on the wrong side of the blanket.

Two more thrusts, and he was done. He tore his mouth from hers and withdrew from her body. The ferocity of his climax took him by surprise. It was like lightning coursing through him, setting him aflame, pleasure rolling up his spine. Gripping his cock, he spent into the bedclothes.

Drained, he collapsed to his back at her side, wishing they never had to leave this bed.

* * *

PART OF MIRABEL—THE wicked part—knew she would inevitably have to leave Damian's bed. But she lingered anyway, reluctant to go. The connection they had shared had been beyond anything she had been prepared for. This had not been a mere joining.

She had lain with her husband before. What had passed between herself and Stanhope bore no comparison to what had occurred between Mirabel and the man who had just taken her to bed.

Transcendent.

That was what it had been. Her heart was still fluttering in her breast, her body humming with the aftereffects of his incredible lovemaking. Lovemaking which had rendered all her previous experience laughable. A disgrace, really.

But she had no notion of how much time she had spent in this haven with Damian Winter, and she had children awaiting her. She was nestled against his chest, breathing in his seductive, masculine scent, her palm flattened over the powerful muscles there. His arm was around her, her head tucked beneath his chin, and his hands were traveling in steady, reassuring passes up and down her back.

Gradually, the ferocity of emotion and sensation subsided. Reality returned, stark and unfortunate. The Duchess of Stanhope could ill afford to take lovers, let alone linger with them above forbidden gaming hells.

She sighed.

"You are thinking about leaving," he predicted, his voice a luscious rumble against her ear.

No sense in prevaricating or prolonging the inescapable.

"Yes," she acknowledged. "My children will be expecting me."

"How many children do you have?"

She hesitated, for speaking about her children whilst she was naked in bed with her lover seemed somehow wrong. But then, there was something different about this man which she could not deny. Something *right*, even when it could not be.

"I have three children," she said at last. "One daughter and two sons. Although they were spending the evening with their aunt and governess, I tell them a tale each night before they go to sleep. I have never missed a night."

Not one. The tradition had begun when Percy had been a babe of no more than two, and he had clung to her as she whispered fantastical tales of knights and magic. It had continued with Joanna when she had been old enough to join in on their sessions, and finally Gideon as well.

"You read to them?"

"No." She smiled, idly rubbing his chest. "I tell them stories which I create as we go along. The tale will never end, I tell them. Each night, we build upon the last."

Creating their mythical world had begun as an escape from the drudgery of her existence. But it had swiftly become a joy when her children had embraced each evening's tale. It was a way for them to bond, to revel in the wonders of a place and people which did not exist.

"You are creating the story together, then?" he asked.

"We are." As Percy had gotten older, he had taken on a greater role in building their world. "I dare not miss it."

"You are a good mother."

Guilt pierced her. "I try. If I were a good mother, I would not be here now."

"You are here for yourself, and there is no shame in that. Long past time you do something for *Mira*, I should think, instead of everyone else."

There he went, making sense. Speaking like a gentleman. Being compassionate. Making her want to linger.

"I love my children, and my duty is to them first," she said.

"If you need to attend them, I understand."

His soft words took her by surprise.

"I do." She felt terribly torn, wanting to stay here another few moments more, and yet knowing she must go. "If I had known... If I had possessed an inkling of what I have been missing..."

Her words trailed off as she realized what she had been about to say and how unfeeling and unkind it was. How much in the vein of the husband she had loathed.

"You would have taken a lover sooner?" Damian asked, once again understanding her far too well. Knowing what she was saying better than she did, it seemed. "I cannot be sorry you did not. I am honored to have been the man to awaken you."

Awaken her. Yes, that was an apt way of describing what he had done tonight, albeit an insufficient one, for mere words were inadequate. She was, however, indeed awake now. And she did not think she could ever go back to sleep.

She wanted more.

She wanted him.

But those were dangerous thoughts, thoughts best kept to herself. Thoughts she would have to banish as surely as she would have to leave his bed.

"I am not sorry about tonight either," she managed to say past the lump rising in her throat. "Thank you."

"No." He kissed the top of her head. "Thank *you*, Mira."

CHAPTER 5

She had returned to Lady Fortune.

Against her better judgment.

Against reason.

In direct opposition to logic.

Damian Winter's smile when he saw her awaiting him at the rear entrance of the establishment made every risk to her reputation worthwhile. When his lips curved upward, the effect of that smoldering grin went straight to all the places he had kissed, licked, and claimed the night before.

"You have come," he said needlessly, taking her hand in his. "I didn't dare believe it was you when Tiny Tom first told me you were here."

Tiny Tom? The gentleman who had greeted her had been a veritable giant. He had been rather fearsome-looking as well. *Good heavens.*

Though she wore her gloves, she felt as if sparks skipped to her elbow beneath Damian's touch. "You asked me to."

"But you are skittish, my lady. Like a newborn foal." He brought her fingers to his lips for a kiss. "I was not certain you would agree."

Being a lover was new to her. Being this particular man's lover was terrifying. Had she overstepped? Was she being too eager? Too forward?

"Shall I go?"

"Hell no, love." He grinned, yanking her into his chest.

His lips were on hers.

She had worn her mask as a precaution, and she was glad for it now as she kissed him back, opening for his tongue. This time, he tasted of tea. Sweet, with a floral note. Intoxicating as ever, despite the absence of the decadent chocolate. Somehow, she had imagined a man such as he would indulge in spirits regularly. It would appear she was wrong.

The longing she had been doing her utmost to keep tamped down unfurled within her. She had risen that morning after a night of feverish dreams, aching and damp. To her shame, Mira had attempted to quell the urges herself, but that had only seemed to heighten her need.

Because nothing could bring her the pleasure this man wrought.

He caught her lower lip in his teeth and tugged, then soothed the sting with his tongue before giving her one final, chaste kiss that left her wanting a dozen more.

Footsteps heralded the arrival of someone, and he stepped away, putting a respectable distance between them as Davy returned. "You're needed in the kitchens, sir," he reported, tugging on his forelock to acknowledge Mirabel. "My Grace."

"Her name is not Grace, lad," Mr. Winter said, frowning.

"Not what I was told," Davy said, puffing up his chest.

Mirabel hoped he would not further give away her identity.

Damian sighed. "What is the matter in the kitchens now, Davy?"

"The boxes for the poor. New Pup got into them and 'ad a

feast. Chef says he doesn't got supplies or time for more boxes."

He muttered an oath beneath his breath. "That dog is going to be the death of me."

Mirabel watched the exchange unfolding, her heart giving a pang. He provided the poor with boxes of food, and he had a dog? Compassion had never been one of Stanhope's virtues. Nor had kindness. And he had absolutely refused to allow her to have any canines in Tarlington House, regardless of how many times she had made the request.

Eventually, she had simply given up on the long-held desire.

"I will be there in a moment," Damian told the boy before turning back to her. "Forgive me, Mira. I am afraid I must take care of this. The men, women, and children of this street depend upon the meals from Lady Fortune. I'll not have them suffer."

He was a good man, she realized. Others in his position would have been only too pleased to keep all their coin for themselves. They would not have been concerned with the plights of those less fortunate.

"I shall help you," she decided.

His frown deepened. "You cannot venture to the kitchens in your fine gown and slippers. They will be ruined."

She shook her head. "I do not intend to help you in the kitchens. I am afraid I would be little aid, having no experience in cooking. However, I can send word to my home. My kitchens can provide whatever extra you require so that your people here do not go hungry."

His frown faded, warmth blazing from his eyes. "You would do that?"

"Of course I would. Why would I not?"

"Many fine ladies don't care to be bothered with the lowly who've hungry bellies."

"I am not many fine ladies," she countered.

He nodded, his admiration warming her heart. "I am beginning to appreciate that."

There was a first—a man who *appreciated* her.

Mirabel bit back her smile, for she had not made the offer to win over Damian Winter. She had made it because it was the right thing to do. "I will send word and have the food brought here. Only tell me what you need."

* * *

She was charming him.

Charming him without trying.

Charming him in a way he had not imagined possible. Demon had always prided himself on his ability to remain unscathed, unaffected. He gambled without compunction. He wooed without thought. He bedded any woman he wanted, and he damn well never wanted her twice.

And yet he, who had never been a fool over a woman before, found himself unable to keep his eyes from Mira or his admiration to himself. He wanted her twice. More than twice. *Good God*, he wanted her again and again and again, without end.

The ferocity of his emotions startled him as he took in the sight of her, still masked, her tresses no longer as immaculate as they had been upon her arrival. Her efforts had sent a few errant wisps down from the knot keeping her hair under control. They framed her face.

She was enchanting, damn her.

They were alone in the kitchens of Lady Fortune, in the wake of a whirlwind effort to fill the boxes for the poor and see them out the door before the hour was too late. Thanks to the plentiful stores which had arrived from her own kitchens, they'd had more than enough to supply the hungry awaiting their nightly dinner on the street.

New Pup had been sent back to Gen, along with her dog Arthur, who was older and much more well-behaved, particularly when bribed with sausages. Davy had gone to bed for the evening. Chef Armande had returned to The Devil's Spawn. The kitchen maids had performed their rigorous cleaning whilst Demon and Mirabel had overseen the packing of the boxes.

Everyone was gone, the hive of bustling activity slowing for the evening.

"Our work here is done," he said softly, leaning his hip against a big wooden table and studying her thoughtfully.

Ever a surprise, this woman.

"I do hope I did not prove a hindrance," she said with a small smile that revealed her even teeth.

When she smiled, it felt as if all the breath had been sucked directly from his lungs. He wanted to kiss her. And bed her. And kiss her some more.

"You were far from a hindrance." He reached out, brushing a tendril of hair on her cheek behind her ear. His hand lingered there. Because now that he was touching her, he did not want to stop. "You were an incredible help. Ordinarily, the packing of the boxes involves Armande shouting, Davy thieving sweets, and the maids tripping over the damned dogs."

Contrary to her earlier declaration that she would be of no use in the kitchens, she had swept within like a general armed with a battle plan. She had hastily organized everyone, from the lowliest scullery to Davy and the chef, giving everyone a task. When the additional food had promptly arrived, she had also orchestrated the dividing of the meals.

Her smile turned shy. "I am accustomed to running a household. Much like being a mother, it requires dedication, determination, organization, and an endless amount of patience."

"I am dedicated and determined," he said, unable to resist caressing her jaw. "Patience, however…I will admit I am lacking."

Especially when it came to her.

He should have bedded her hours ago. He should have been inside her by now. At the least, his tongue should be on her slick, responsive pearl.

But she had fretted over people she had never met. People whose paths she would never cross. And she had been hell-bent upon seeing them all fed.

"You have been patient enough with me," she said, voice low.

She was referring to her lack of experience, he knew.

"I can be when it is required of me." He stepped nearer, breathing in the headiness of her scent, above the familiar smells of the kitchens. "And especially when the reward is worth the wait."

"Oh."

She was flustered. He wanted to see her pink cheeks. Her shyness was deuced sweet. All the lovers he'd had in the past had been bold, sure of themselves. He liked the hint of vulnerability she could not always hide.

Idly, he tugged at the ties of her mask. "May I take this off?"

Her gaze cast about the room, as if suspecting an interloper to suddenly appear.

"You are safe here, with me," he assured her. "No one will see you. They are all through with their duties for the night, and Tiny Tom will still be overseeing the floor until it is time to lock the doors for the evening."

She nodded. "If you wish."

Thank Christ.

He plucked at the knot and whisked the cursed thing away. Somehow, it was a sign of the anonymity which lingered between them. A taunt he did not like. A reminder that for all the intimacies they had shared yesterday, she had only seen fit to trust him with her Christian name. Not a title. Nothing more.

He tucked the mask inside his coat, wishing it to perdition but knowing he must save it for later, when she would go. "Thank you for helping us. The hour grows late. Do your children not need you this evening?"

Her flush heightened. "I told them their story earlier tonight, just as I have done when I had other social engagements in the past."

Balls and such, he supposed she meant. The reminder of the differences between them was unwelcome. Here in the low light of the kitchens, no one about save the two of them, it was almost easy to believe the fancy that they were equals. That she did not belong to an unforgiving world of wealth and importance, the same world his sister Gen could not allow to reveal the truth. Bad enough society knew her to be a bastard Winter. But if they knew she also owned and secretly ran Lady Fortune, the same lords and ladies who now whispered about her would turn their backs entirely.

No sense, however, in wasting what precious time he had with Mira on wishing their circumstances were any different. He could not change who he was any more than she could.

"You will stay for a time?" He was still absentmindedly stroking her jaw, reluctant to sever their connection.

He trailed his knuckles lightly down the column of her throat, his fingers toying with the gold and glittering stones on the necklace of her parure. She was a wealthy woman, his Mira, whoever she was.

"Do you wish me to?" she asked, her voice a throaty invitation.

"Christ yes, love. I assume that is the reason you arrived earlier and not so you could ruin your slippers and fret over boxes in my kitchens."

She smiled. "It is good of you, feeding those in need."

He shrugged. "It was my partner's idea."

That was not entirely true. He and Gen had come upon the solution together. Lady Fortune was on the edge of the East End, in a place near enough to where nobs made their homes that wealthy ladies felt safe. However, it was still the East End. There had been many beggars on the streets. Many in need. Using their extra food each evening to help feed the hungry was one way Lady Fortune helped the street upon which it stood.

"You have a partner?" Mira's eyebrows rose.

"A secret partner," he said quickly. "One who does not wish to be known."

"A woman?" she asked.

"What of you? Would you care to tell me your full name?"

Her lush lips tightened. "Touché, sir."

He tamped down his disappointment. Of course she would not reveal her identity to him. She guarded her privacy well, and although he knew Davy had been to her home, Demon had respected her right to maintain her anonymity and he had not pressed the lad for further information.

"Why are we lingering in the kitchens when we could be in my bed?" he asked, seeking to distract them both from the grimness of reality.

"Why indeed?"

He cupped her nape, drawing her to him for a kiss. She made a soft sound of surrender, her arms going around his neck, and her lips moved against his with greater confidence than she had kissed him before. When her tongue tentatively traced the seam of his lips, he groaned. She was a quick student.

He thought about all the things he could teach her, and his cock went stiffer than a poker in his trousers. Their tongues slid together. He wanted more. This half measure was not nearly enough.

He tore his lips from hers. "I need you, Mira."

The fringe of her lashes swept over her brilliant eyes, shielding them from him. "I need you, too."

The best four words he had ever damned well heard. "Come, love."

* * *

For the second night in a row, Mirabel found herself trespassing inside the territory of Mr. Damian Winter.

Octavia had told her to come here. Had promised to see the children to bed on her behalf.

Go, her sister had said. *You deserve to have something that makes you happy.*

I am happy, she had argued stoically.

Something aside from Percy, Joanna, and Gideon, Octavia had countered. *You seem so happy today, darling. So unlike yourself. Go and forget what it means to be the Duchess of Stanhope, even if for the evening. Go and see him.*

Octavia had not needed to explain who she was speaking of.

When Mirabel had returned home last night, flushed and disheveled and unable to keep from smiling, her sister had taken one look at her and *known*. It was the sisterly bond they shared—an ability to communicate without requiring words. Also, the compassion to want the best for each other, without fear of guilt or recrimination. Octavia would never censure her for taking Damian Winter as a lover.

Still, despite Octavia's urgings, Mirabel knew this madness she was engaging in could not last. It had been doomed from the start. But what was the harm in reveling in it, if just for the night? If just while it lasted?

Tonight, she wanted to take her time. To savor every moment, take note of each detail. Later, when this was over, she would be able to remember everything—the way he had made her feel, the way his scent had wafted over her, the feeling of his fingers entwined with hers, the pounding of her heart, the heady desire throbbing to life within. She cast her eyes about the chamber, taking note of the shelf of books, which pleased and surprised her, the writing desk in tidy order, the quill in its well.

"Does my lady approve?"

The low rumble of his voice sent a shiver down her spine.

She glanced back at him, thinking it unfair a man could be so wickedly handsome. "Of course."

"You are cold?" he asked with a frown, as if the thought displeased him. "I'll build the fire."

"No." She laid a staying hand on his coat sleeve, stopping him. "I am not cold."

Indeed, she was quite the opposite. She was hot. And aching for him.

He studied her. "Tell me something, Mira."

"What would you have me tell you?"

She waited, wondering what he would ask. Wondering if it was a question she dared answer.

"The first night you came here, looking for a lover," he said. "Why did you do it? For a lady such as yourself, one with little experience, engaging the aid of a stranger seems a risk. Especially for a woman so concerned about maintaining her secrecy."

He was not wrong.

Her cheeks were hot. "My sister suggested the madcap scheme. I cannot say I should have listened. Apparently, she based her knowledge upon caricatures, the scandal broadsides sold each day."

"Octavia," he said, startling her at the direct mentioning of her sister.

How alarming it seemed, coming from his lips. How personal in a way nothing they had shared thus far had been.

"How do you know her name?" she demanded, instantly pulling up her guard.

"You mentioned her that night. *I told Octavia coming here was a mistake*, you said."

Her distrust deflated. Drat the man and his memory. So she had.

"I said I didn't know who Octavia was but that I was sure you being here wasn't a mistake," he continued, untying the knot on his cravat as he watched her with that dark, intent stare of his. The one that made her feel all quivery inside. "Then you said—"

"Never mind who Octavia is," she interrupted. "That is what I said. I recall now well enough."

He pulled his cravat from around his neck and tossed it upon the carpets, then began shrugging out of his coat. "I offered to be your lover, and you told me to go to the devil."

Shame stung her. "I never told you to go to the devil."

"May as well have done." His coat fell to the floor. "I ain't holding it against you, love. You've recognized the error of your ways."

Somehow, his suddenly rough speech, in such disparity with his often smooth, gentlemanly drawl, did not bother her. If anything, it heightened her longing. She watched, breathless, as he opened the buttons on his dark waistcoat. He shrugged the garment away, and she found herself mesmerized by the breadth of his chest in his crisp white shirt. By the expanse of his throat on display, the masculine prominence of his Adam's apple. By his long fingers flicking open the line of three buttons at the neck of his shirt.

He had said something, had he not?

Oh, was it her turn to speak?

Any chance of her offering a response was severely diminished when he grasped his shirt and hauled it over his head. His chest was glorious. Yesterday, in their frenzy, she had not taken the proper time to admire him. They had been an eager tangle of limbs, and her recollections were a blur of passion and desire as the two of them had divested him of his garments. Now, she had the chance to take him in.

And take him in, she did. He was lean and strong, his chest covered in a smattering of dark hair, his stomach taut. Stanhope had never bothered to remove his dressing gown. Often, he had come to her wearing his night cap. But his body had not been at all similar in composition; he had been rendered soft by years of leisure and indulgence. There was nothing soft about Damian Winter.

Nothing at all.

And the rigid protrusion against the fall of his trousers was adamant proof of that.

"You are staring, Mira."

Hot and flustered, she jerked her gaze away from the evidence of his desire, meeting his dark eyes. "Forgive me. It is merely that I am…you are…"

He held out his hand. "Come here."

She went. What else was there to do? She was drawn to him, helplessly, hopelessly, deliciously. Her hand settled in his. Sparks flew past her elbow, then radiated elsewhere, landing between her thighs.

"You are lovely," he said softly, tugging at the tips of her glove and pulling it off.

She swallowed.

He brought her bare hand to his chest, settling it over his heart. "Touch me as you like, love."

His skin was warm. His scent washed over her. She absorbed the steady thumping of his life source. "I like touching you."

His mouth kicked up in a sensual grin. "And I like when you touch me."

She remained frozen as she was, wanting to explore more of him and yet hesitant. A sudden shyness swept over her. Being intimate with a man was so new to her. No matter how many times Stanhope had lain with her, it had never been close to this. Instead, it had been impersonal and polite, uncomfortable and hasty and awkward. Stanhope had been raised to believe pleasure was to be found with his mistress alone and that his duchess was purely for the purpose of siring heirs. Mirabel had been raised to believe the same, but that had not stopped her from longing for more.

So many wasted years.

At long last, passion was here, hers for the taking.

Damian reached for her other hand, pulling it free of the kid glove as well, before drawing her other palm to his chest. Such barely contained strength. He was so masculine. So forbidden.

So...*hers*.

At least for the night. For the next few hours before she had to return to her life as the staid, always proper Duchess of Stanhope.

Hesitantly, she caressed him. The dichotomy of smooth, warm flesh and coarse masculine hair delighted her. He was beautiful. She never wanted the night to end. Never wanted this connection between them to sever, though she knew it inevitably would.

"You are wearing far too many layers," he grumbled, his

fingers going to work on the fastenings at the back of her gown.

She thrilled at the frustration in his deep voice. For the first time, she became aware of her effect upon him, realizing this attraction was not one-sided. That she possessed far more power than she had understood last night in her wild state of desire.

Feeling bold, she caressed down his chest, over the firm, muscled slab of his abdomen. Then lower, to the waistband of his trousers. When she neared the fall, where his manhood stood in prominent relief, he caught her wrist.

"Naughty minx." He kissed her swiftly. "I want you naked first, or I won't last long enough."

Together, they worked her out of her gown and all the rest of her trappings. Her slippers were likely ruined, but she did not care. She would ruin them again if given the chance. What she felt for him was wild and dangerous, reckless and wrong.

And yet, it would not be stopped.

Not as he kissed every bare expanse of flesh he revealed. Not as he led her to the bed. Not even as he took up his discarded cravat and met her gaze.

"Do you want me, Mira?"

His low query settled over her like warm silk. "Yes."

"How much?" He kissed her throat.

"Too much." The truth was torn from her.

"I like you this way," he murmured as his teeth raked over her neck. "Nude except for your jewels, like a sinful queen."

She shivered again, and once more, it had nothing to do with being chilled. "Oh."

He nuzzled her ear. "I want you on my bed, naked and waiting for me."

Somehow, she found the strength to walk to his bed and drape herself upon it as he had asked. Beneath the scrutiny of his dark, heated gaze, she was aflame. She felt, for the first time, truly free. Aware of her independence from her husband's rule. At liberty to do what she pleased, with whomever she desired.

And now, the man she desired was watching her with an expression that said he wanted to devour her. Watching her as he removed his boots and strode toward the end of the bed. She was acutely aware of every sensation—the feather pillows at her back, the soft fabric of the counterpane, the thud of her own heartbeat, the languorous heat sliding through her, the wetness between her thighs.

"I like the way you look here better," he declared. "Take down your hair for me."

The command in his voice made her hungrier for him. She liked being his woman. Liked being Mira.

This is only temporary, warned the voice within. *You cannot continue seeing this man. Scandal will inevitably follow.*

But she ignored the voice, reaching for the pins in her hair. One by one, she plucked them free, tossing them to the floor as she went. Locks fell around her shoulders, down her back.

"Yes," he said, his voice husky. "Christ, your hair is beautiful. It is like flame. But then, so are you."

"How can I be like flame?" she dared to ask, mesmerized by the unabashed hunger in his countenance, the way he consumed her with his stare.

"Flame is beautiful." His fingers were on the fall of his trousers, undoing buttons from their moorings now. "It is necessary for life, yet dangerous. Watch its beauty from afar, hastily run your finger through it and you will be unscathed, but if you linger too long, you will be burned."

"I shall not burn you," she whispered, watching as he lowered his trousers and his manhood sprang forth, stiff and long and thick.

"Do you promise?"

She tossed the last pin from her hair. "I promise."

He joined her on the bed, his warmth and strength pinning her there. She caught his face in her hands and brought his lips to hers for a kiss that quickly deepened, growing carnal. His fingers dipped between their bodies, and she could not contain her moan when he found that same, sensitive flesh, stroking her with expert precision.

"Christ, Mira. You're so wet and ready for me, aren't you?"

"Always." It was the truth. No sense in hiding it; his fingers were on her, knowing. She did not think she could ever get enough of this man. Did not think there would ever come a day when he did not bring her to her knees with wanting him.

Her hips jerked, seeking more. Her fingers tunneled through his hair.

He toyed with her, stroking, circling the bud with confident caresses that brought her easily near to the edge. But just when she thought she might come entirely undone, he retreated, his touch gliding lower. Parting her folds before delving into her aching center.

Two fingers, then a third. He sucked on her throat, his rigid cock pressed to her hip as he pleasured her, reaching an incredibly sensitized place. So sensitive, the lines between pleasure and pain seemed to blur. But still, she wanted more. Wantonly, she planted her heels on the counterpane and surged upward, taking those fingers deeper still.

He kissed a path to her breasts, then took a nipple in his mouth and sucked hard. His thumb found the bud of her sex, swirling over it and heightening her desperation. He flicked his tongue over the peak of her breast, then gently bit as he thrust his fingers in and out of her, thumb working, rotating, massaging.

She cried out, body convulsing, channel tightening on him. Bliss hit her with such force that tiny black stars speckled her vision. But just when she thought she could not bear any more, he kissed lower, fingers still buried within her. Kissed down her stomach, all the way to her mound. When his lips replaced his thumb, all the air fled her lungs.

It was as if he was intent upon taking her to the point of mindlessness. But after having spent all her life in the dearth of desire, beneath the sovereignty of a man who had never cared if she found any pleasure at all in the act of lovemaking, she could not say she minded. Damian Winter was everything she could have wanted in a lover and more than she had imagined.

He licked and sucked, his wicked tongue traveling over her most intimate flesh as his long fingers stretched and slid, bringing her once more to the brink. As he gently nibbled on her and crooked his fingers, she came apart. Wildly. Splendidly.

A rush of wetness flooded from her, and she shook and writhed and gasped. It was as if her entire being had seized. As if she were dipped in gold and flame. She felt every bit the sinful queen he had told her she resembled. He made her feel that way. He made her feel as if she were worthy of pleasure, of his regard. Made her feel as if he worshiped her body.

He stayed with her as the last waves of pleasure faded, before he flipped to his back, pulling her with him so that she was astride his big body, her hips on either side of his. His thick cock jutted between them, nestled against her aching folds.

She stared down at Damian, her palms flattened on his chest as she sought purchase in her precarious new position atop him. And she found she rather enjoyed this position of power.

"I want you to ride me, love," he said. "You control the lovemaking. I am all yours."

All yours.

Oh, how she wished he was indeed hers. Longing lanced through her, fervent and painful at once. He could never be hers. Not truly. Nor could she be his. They could pretend, however. They could seize this moment and each other and make the most of this furious desire whilst it lasted.

"Tell me what to do," she said, uncertain despite her enjoyment at being the one who would decide upon their pace and pleasure.

He grasped his rigid staff, running the blunt head over her sensitized pearl.

"Mmm." She could not quell the moan of delight that rose from her.

"Lift yourself," he said, voice thick and low with longing.

She rose on her knees obediently.

He aligned himself with her, the tip of his cock brushing against her entrance. "Take what you want, Mira."

His gruff urging was all the impetus she required. She sank down upon his straining member, slowly at first and then with greater intent. Until he was lodged inside her, deep and thick and pulsing.

"Dear God," she said, the pleasure so intense, she found herself crumpling against his hard chest.

"We've had this talk before, love. Not God." He grinned up at her, his hands grasping her waist in a grip that was somehow possessive and tender. "Just Demon Winter."

"Damian," she corrected him, because she did not like Demon.

It made him sound evil instead of wonderful.

"Damian Winter then," he allowed. "Still not the Lord. Not a lord at all. Just a bastard."

"Hush." Mira pressed a hand to his lips, her finger settling in the perfect dip of his philtrum. "You are not *just* anything."

He kissed her forefinger. "Then ride me, my girl. Have me however you want me."

She did not know what he meant, though she was willing to learn. He seemed to understand her hesitance, for his hands tightened on her waist, gently guiding her up and down. He allowed her to find the pace she wanted, just as he had promised.

Making love in this position was intense, not just because her body regulated their mutual pleasure, but because there was no hiding from the carnality of the act. She was on him, taking him in slow and steady plunges, her hips finding the rhythm her body needed, rocking into him again and again. Her breasts were bare and bouncing. His eyes were dark and intense on hers. Soon, slow and steady was not enough.

She needed faster. Harder. Deeper.

She planted her hands on the pillow at either side of his beautiful face, and she worked harder, trying to find the next release her body so desperately required. He spurred her on every moment of the way.

"Yes, Mira. Harder. Ride my cock."

His shocking words had their intended effect. She did everything he asked, closing her eyes as she gave herself up to the intensity of the sensations. Her hair cascaded down her back. The wet sounds of their lovemaking filled his chamber. No moment in her life had ever been more erotic.

"Like this?" she managed to taunt him as she moved with greater confidence.

"Yes." He groaned, hips working beneath her to drive himself higher, deeper. "Just like that. Fuck me, love."

Vulgar words from a lowborn man. He had been born to a different class. She had been born to be a duke's wife, to snare the coronet her mother had wanted for her. And she had done her duty all this time, had lived above reproach. If anyone who knew the Duchess of Stanhope could see her now, they would have been disgusted.

And Mirabel herself? She should have been shocked. Horrified. She should be mired in so much shame that she would never again find her way to Lady Fortune or to this man's arms and bed.

Except she knew she was going to do so.

Again.

And again.

And again.

As often as she could. Because she wanted this man as she had never wanted another. And because after so many painful years of being the submissive, passionless duchess she had been forced to be, she deserved this man. Deserved this desire, this passion, this uncontrollable flame.

She rode him harder, seeking her crisis. It was near, so near. He caught her breast in his mouth, sucking hard on her nipple, and that was it. She lost herself completely, shattering and splintering, coming so hard, she screamed.

Through the thundering of her own heart, she scarcely heard his warning.

"Damn, Mira, I'm going to come."

But she was selfish, and she did not want to put an end to their joining. So she remained where she was, atop him, astride him, his cock lodged deep as the hot spurt of his seed filled her.

CHAPTER 6

"You are lovely as always this evening, Mira," Damian told her.

Was it a sin that she loved her name on his lips, spoken thus—as if it were a prayer?

She had come back to Lady Fortune every night for nearly a fortnight. Of course she had, for it was impossible to stay away from him. He was intoxicating. He was everything she could never have, and he was hers for these glorious, stolen moments in the freedom of his apartments. Here, she was free to be his lover. She was not Mirabel. Not the Duchess of Stanhope. Not mother, sister, not a prim pillar of society.

She was only Mira, herself as she had always longed to be. And she was with him, this sinful, wonderful man with the charming rogue's smile and the cocky swagger. The man who owned every room he inhabited with the sheer magnetism of his presence.

This can never last, whispered the voice of doubt within.

She hated that voice. And for now, she chose to ignore it.

"Thank you," she told him softly, taking the opportunity to admire him in return.

And oh, was he a sight to behold. His hair was tousled, falling at a rakish angle over his brow, his eyes glittering in the candlelight. He was dressed in a navy coat and matching cravat, a waistcoat of ivory and buff trousers, his booted feet indolently crossed at the ankles.

They were lounging on the floor in a nest of pillows he had created for them, surrounded by a spread of wine, strawberries, and honey cakes. Damian had enquired after whether or not she had dined that evening. In her eagerness to be with him, she had not. With Percy, Joanna, and Gideon otherwise being looked after so she could do her duty and attend the Evesham ball, she had taken advantage of her freedom. After making her obligatory appearance, she had offered her excuses and escaped, coming to Lady Fortune before the revelers had proceeded to dinner.

The supper boxes already having gone out for the night, Damian had scoured the kitchens for some remainders himself. She had awaited him in his private room, taking the time to investigate its interior. She wanted to know more about this man.

Everything there was to know. What made him smile? What caused him to laugh? How many siblings did he have? Had he ever been married before? Had he loved?

"You are serious tonight," he observed, cutting through the silence which had fallen between them. "Is it because I have lured you away from your elegant ball and now you have discovered all I have to offer is some paltry sweets and a bottle of Madeira?"

He was teasing, but there was an undercurrent in his voice, one she did not think she misunderstood. A note of uncertainty. And she could hardly fault him; he had gone out of his way to entertain her this evening, and she was sitting in the midst of his splendor, frowning away.

"Forgive me." She accepted the wine he held out for her, their bare fingers brushing and sending a wave of awareness washing over her. "I am not at all disappointed by your sweets, your wine, or yourself. Indeed, I am quite pleased. Too pleased, really. There is nowhere else I should rather be just now, nor any other person I should wish to be with."

"You pay me a great compliment, my lady." He raised his glass to her in toast. "I feel the same."

Guilt gnawed at her. She should tell him her true identity, that she was the Duchess of Stanhope. Whenever he called her *my lady*, she entertained the briefest fancy that someone else was in the room with them.

But there was far too much at stake. Her children depended upon her to be circumspect, to make the right decisions. How little she knew of this man, regardless of how well she knew his body.

And so instead of revealing all, she toasted him in return before raising her glass to her lips for a delicate sip. The Madeira was of excellent quality, its flavor lush and full on her tongue. She took a moment to savor it. To savor the quiet of the room, the potential of the night. They had hours ahead of them.

Still, it did not seem enough.

She swallowed. "I cannot help but to feel it is you who pays me a compliment."

Wryly, she reminded herself of the difference in age between them. She was ten years older than he, with three children.

"Perhaps we are evenly matched in this, if nothing else." He flashed her his rascal's grin, his charm making her heart pound faster. "May I fashion you a plate?"

As always, his manners were impeccable. His speech, if

not flawlessly accented, devilishly attractive. There was something about the combination of polished charm and rough East End strut that filled her with fire.

"Thank you. That would be lovely."

She sipped some more of her Madeira, admiring his long, masculine fingers as he set about arranging fruit and cake on a plate for her. His nails were trimmed and neat. And she knew how those fingers felt on her. In her.

Exquisite.

Her nipples tightened and the ache in her core would not be ignored. But now was not the time. Her stomach was every bit as needy as the rest of her.

"Your repast, such as it is, milady," he intoned in mocking formal accents, as if he were attempting to imitate an august butler.

She took the plate he offered, unable to tamp down her smile. "Thank you, kind sir. However shall I express my gratitude?"

He winked. "I have a notion or two."

As did she. Warmth suffused her, adding to the heat that always seemed to emanate from him. But she wanted to prolong their time together. She could not justify coming to him so early in the evening, for most days she did not have a ball with which she could disguise her nighttime visits. Her children needed her, especially Percy, who would soon be off to school.

How she dreaded the day when she would no longer call upon Damian. When she would have to put the inevitable end to this idyll they shared. But then she reminded herself sternly that when she had first come upon the notion of taking a lover, well before she had ever met Damian Winter, she had known her time of recklessness would have to be finite. One could not play with fire forever without getting burned.

She took a bite of her honey cake. It was crumbly, sweet, and divine on her tongue. Chef Armande was to be commended for his efforts. Mirabel could not quite suppress her moan of appreciation, impossibly dreadful manners though she knew such an act was. There was something about being with the man before her that set her free from all the damning strictures that had forced her to be so rigidly proper.

The years ceased to exist.

So, too, the loneliness.

How was it that he made her feel as if she had always known him, as if she could scarcely recall what her life had been like before he had been a part of it? And her having known him such a scant amount of time. It was unheard of.

"Does my lady approve?" he asked with a tender smile.

She approved of far more than the cakes and fruits. Far more than the wine.

Mirabel swallowed, mustering a smile of her own. "It is delicious. Thank you. It is not every day that a gentleman is so intent upon sating my hunger."

The moment the words fled her, she realized the double entendre she had not intended. Her cheeks were scalding hot.

He flashed her a cocky grin, one that said he did not take offense to her words one bit. "Dare I hope I am the only gentleman so intent upon sating you?"

She bit her lip, struggling to regain her composure. "I was referring to the other sort of hunger, Mr. Winter."

He raised a brow, so confident and handsome that it required all her self-restraint to keep from throwing herself into his lap and taking those sensual lips with hers.

"Is there another sort of hunger?" he quipped.

"There is and you know it."

"Enlighten me."

He was teasing her. Taunting her. The air in the room became suddenly heavy. Laden with desire. Their gazes clashed and held.

"Which hunger was it *you* were speaking of?" she asked.

"The pangs gnawing your stomach, of course," he said with a gallant air. "I would like to think myself the only man concerned with whether or not you have dined."

He was.

But he was also pushing her.

Making her feel flushed, vulnerable, and awakened.

"You are the only man," she managed. "Just as I have promised. The only man who frets over my dinner and the only man who frets over my pleasure."

His grin was wide and so attractive she forgot to breathe. "That is good to hear, love. But satisfy your stomach first. I'll not pleasure you when you've an empty belly."

Her stomach growled as if to concur. She sent him a small smile and returned her attention to the plate he had arranged, making short work of the consumption of her honey cakes and strawberries both, along with two glasses of wine along the way. Midway through their repast, they began a game in which they asked each other questions.

She had already learned he had eleven siblings. He enjoyed singing and throwing knives. He was an expert marksman and a self-described middling prizefighter. His brother Mr. Gavin Winter was an undisputed champion in that arena. The notion of Damian facing anyone with his fists made Mirabel ill. It seemed such a dangerous, aggressive sport. His favorite sister was named Gen, though he also loved his five other sisters, who were legitimate Winters. He had excellent luck at the tables. He had never been wed, and nor had he any children.

For her part, she had confessed to Damian that she was one of five children—four daughters and one son. Her elder sisters had married, although not as well as she had. Here, she spared the details of her having become the Duchess of Stanhope. Her younger sister had never wed, and she was Mirabel's closest friend and beloved confidante.

"Octavia is the unwed sister, then, I trust," Damian guessed.

She was impressed he possessed none of the accompanying disgust which ordinarily accompanied the knowledge that a woman had failed to marry.

Then again, perhaps that was only Mirabel's mother who possessed that particular disgust.

"She made a wise decision," Mirabel said. "Married women possess no rights. She is free to live with me as long as she likes, and there is no one to treat her cruelly or to tell her what she must and must not do."

Damian stilled. "If he were alive, I would call him out."

The vehemence in his voice left no question. He was speaking of Stanhope.

"But if he were alive, I never would have met you," she pointed out, casting her mostly empty plate aside. A few strawberries lolled on the porcelain. "I would never have dared to come to a place like Lady Fortune, or to meet with a man like you, when my husband was alive. The repercussions would have been too damning."

They still could be, which was why she took care with her identity. Though it felt increasingly like a burden she carried about.

"Did he beat you?" Damian asked, the question stark and bitter.

"He hit me sometimes," she admitted. "Especially when we were first wed. I was not… He told me I was not biddable as I must be."

She had learned quickly how to conduct herself to avoid inciting her husband's wrath. She had fashioned herself into the perfect duchess. One who did everything the duke required of her, never questioned him, offered an opinion, or did anything that would bring shame upon his family name.

"Fuck him." Damian's abrupt words, cutting through the silence, were guttural. Filled with venom. His eyes were on her, dark and intent. "He did not deserve you."

The depth of his emotion took her by surprise. And humbled her. Made her eyes burn with suppressed tears. Octavia had told her as much, but hearing it from Damian was somehow different.

She swallowed. "Thank you."

"No thanking me." He was on his knees, crawling toward her now, over the pillows he had mounded on the floor, not stopping until there was no more distance remaining between them. "Do not thank me for observing the truth, the obvious. Your husband was a shit sack. And now, I must make amends."

She would have laughed at the term *shit sack* had he not been so serious. So genuine. Her heart pounded. He reached her, still on all fours, and pressed his lips to hers. Her arms wound around his neck, holding him to her. He caught her lower lip in his teeth and gently tugged. Passion was a lustrous, heady warmth, snaking through her. Filling her with a strange sense of euphoria.

Mirabel bit him back, nipping at the full succulence of his lower lip in the same fashion as he had done to her. Her hands tugged at his hair. She wanted the heaviness of his lean, muscular body atop hers, wanted the divine sensation of him entering her, filling and stretching her. She wanted to inhale his scent every moment of every day, impossible as it was. They had spent their nights together in a frenzied blur of bliss, but still, his every action only made her desire him a hundred times more.

"On your back, Mira," he growled against her lips.

It was not a request but a command. She did as he asked, settling herself upon the pillows. The soft, feathery mounds contoured to her body. She scarcely knew she was upon the floor—there was no hardness beneath her. She felt, instead, as if she were inhabiting a cloud.

Damian moved until he was situated at her feet, where her ankles were yet pressed firmly together. She lay there as he had asked, watching him, trusting him.

She opened her legs for him without his request or gentle guidance, knowing all too well the pleasure to be had at this beautiful man's hands. Her gown lifted, her petticoat and chemise traveling along. The coolness of the late-spring air, tempered only by the glow of the low fire in the hearth, glanced over her most intimate flesh. Her skirts went higher still, all the way to her waist. Mirabel allowed her legs to fall farther apart. His eyes fell hungrily upon the skin she had revealed to him.

She felt not a bit of shame as his hands closed on her ankles, gliding up her calves. Not a speck of embarrassment as he murmured sweet praises to her and kissed his way past her knees. His mouth was a hot, welcome brand upon her bare flesh when he traveled beyond her garters and stockings.

If he was going to feast upon her as if she were the food they had just consumed, he would find no complaints from her. Indeed, she longed for the soft flick of his tongue over her most intimate flesh once more. He pressed a kiss to her inner thigh, getting ever nearer to her pulsing, aching center.

His head lifted. He plucked a strawberry from her abandoned porcelain plate on the carpets.

She watched in rapt fascination and confusion, wondering what he intended to do. Indulge in dessert? Pleasure her? As it happened, she did not have long to wait or wonder, for his head dipped low, and he kissed a trail up her right thigh, all the way to her mound. He kissed her there, lightly, gently, almost as if it were scarcely a kiss at all.

His tongue flicked over the throbbing bud of her sex. But then, he left her, kissing the inside of her left thigh, and in place of his mouth upon her bud, she felt instead the light brush of something curved and plump, its surface studded with an unusual texture. It brushed over her pearl, manipulating her with light pressure. Not nearly enough.

Her hips thrust, a sigh leaving her. He was being too gentle. Too soft. She wanted more. Harder. She wanted his tongue, but she also wanted his manhood, stiff and long as she knew him to be, deep inside her.

"Be calm, Mira, else you shall mangle my dessert," Damian said, his sinful baritone cutting through the calm stillness of the room.

Before she could say a thing in response, he kissed her thigh before returning to his task. He sucked as if she were the most delicious dish he had ever sampled and he needed to savor her now lest he was never again afforded the opportunity to taste her. As before, the pleasure was intense. Blissful.

He licked her. "Are you ready, love?"

She would have answered, but she could not speak, for he had once more begun to stimulate her. He was driving her wild. Her hips bucked against him as she sought more. More pressure, harder, faster, more *him*.

He slid the berry between her lower lips. His mouth closed over her pearl, sucking at the same instant he slid the strawberry inside her. Not the entire fruit, but the bulbous end of it, whilst his lips and teeth and tongue brought her to the brink. He sucked and gently thrust the berry into her channel. She was slick, pulsing, so ready for him. In and out, he thrust the fruit, until she was sure it was coated in her essence.

She ought to be ashamed and she knew it. This display, her on her back, legs spread for him to feast upon her as if he were a starving man, her body undulating mindlessly against his mouth and tongue. The berry. *Dear, sweet Lord in heaven*, the strawberry. He had lodged it inside her passage now, stretching her, and left it where it was before throwing his entire attention into pleasuring the highly sensitive, engorged bud of her sex.

He caught her between his teeth and tugged, then sucked so hard and long, worshiping her hungry flesh as if she were a goddess and he was pledging his allegiance to her. She did not miss the reverence in his touch, in his kiss, his caress.

She moaned and thrust her hips from the pillows, her heels digging into the carpet, woolen and solid beneath her. He was lashing her pearl with his tongue now, then nipping her once more, and sucking. Sucking so hard, so long, so deliciously, she could not…her spend was inevitable. She gave in. Her body was like one tightly drawn knot, cinching, bringing her ever closer, and the waves of delirious pleasure were pounding upon her until she could not resist. She shook, her pinnacle rocking through her with the force of an earthquake.

Damian's face was buried between her thighs, his tongue continuing to expertly tease her pearl while his finger sank inside her, joining the strawberry as the last tremors fled her. He pulled it from her, raising his head. His expression was a gift, slack with pleasure, unguarded and vulnerable. His beautiful mouth was reddened and slick with her own juices.

She swallowed against a wild rush of pleasure at the sight. At her mark upon him. He licked his lips beneath her scrutiny, as if he reveled in every last drop of her. As she looked on with helpless fascination, he lifted the strawberry he had used to pleasure her to his lips. His teeth bit into it.

"Delicious," he said.

Oh, he was wicked.

And oh, how she loved that wickedness. How she longed to bask in it. To bask in him.

Always. It was as if his intensity poured into her soul, and it remained there. She knew she could not remove it now, not even if she wished to do so. Damian Winter was a part of her, so deep and so true he could never be removed. Not from her heart, not from her memories, and not from her life.

Nor did she want him to be. Even if this time they had was fleeting, and even if she knew they could not remain lovers forever, being with him had changed her irrevocably.

Another urge struck her. The urge to make him reach his pinnacle the same way he had just brought her to wild, blissful release.

With her mouth.

"I want to bring you pleasure," she told him. "It is your turn."

"No, love, this was for you," he returned, chasing her pronouncement with his lips.

As they kissed, the muskiness of her and the sweet tartness of the strawberry mingled. It was forbidden and potent and she wanted him more than she could have imagined. The effect this man had upon her was dangerous.

*** * * ***

Floating hell, the effect Mira had upon him…

Demon was out of his mind with wanting her. She was ruining him for any other woman. Mayhap she already had. Everything about her was intoxicating, and it spoke to him on a different level. He spent all the time they were apart thinking of her, longing for her, counting the bloody minutes until he knew she would arrive. This evening, she had been an hour late on account of some social engagement. The wait had seemed an eternity.

He slowed the kiss, need clamoring through him with a fury that would not be denied. Her lips curved in a smile as he dragged them over hers, and he loved how she did that, as if they were sharing a secret. And in a way, he supposed they were. He was her secret lover. He still did not know her true identity, and it was likely that he never would.

Demon did not know why the notion should cause a pang in his heart, but it did.

One which he could do nothing about.

So he tamped it down and set about the task of stripping Mira bare. She was dressed in a white gown that set off her bold tresses and blue eyes in a way that had made him long to take her up in his arms and carry her away the moment he had first seen her earlier that evening. He took great care in removing the fine, embroidered gown now with her aid. Next came her stays, petticoat, and chemise. Her slippers and stockings, he saved for last, relishing the sight of her, all lush curves and beautiful femininity in a sea of pillows.

"Damn it, woman, you are perfect." He punctuated his pronouncement with kisses to the skin he had revealed.

Starting with her ankles, then up her calves. Higher. To her knees, his mouth settling in the sweetly scented hollow there. She shivered beneath him, moving as if she could not contain her eagerness.

"I am far from perfect," she told him on a breathless gasp as he found her thighs and urged them wider apart.

She allowed them to fall open, giving him the perfect view of her pink flesh, glistening from the pleasure he had already given her, the plump, pouting bud of her sex calling for his lips and tongue and teeth once more.

He was rigid, hard as an iron poker.

"How wrong you are, love," he managed to rasp,

worshiping her as he went. Over her hip. To her belly, where she was curved and soft, so soft. He kissed the indentation, then dragged his mouth to her breast. "You are all that is lovely and feminine and beautiful."

"You make me feel beautiful," she murmured, clutching at his shoulders as he sucked her nipple.

He released it, pressing a kiss to the plump side of her breast. "You should feel beautiful. Because you are."

And damn her idiotic husband for making her think anything less. The man ought to have been drowned in the Thames for the manner in which he had treated her, withholding passion from her, making her feel as if she were anything less than the astounding, lushly feminine goddess she was. *Hurting her. Damnation*, he wished he could avenge her pain.

"I am far too old to be beautiful," she protested as he kissed his way to her neck.

He settled between her thighs and realized, quite belatedly, that he was still fully clothed. *Damn it*, this was becoming a regular problem when he was in her presence.

Demon leveraged himself over her on one elbow, using his free hand to cup her face. "Look at me, Mira. You are not too old to be beautiful. You could never be too old. Indeed, I'll wager everything I possess that when you are gray-haired, you will be every bit as beautiful as you are now. Every bit as tempting."

"Damian." She said his name on a sigh. "You always know what to say."

He rubbed his thumb over her lower lip. "Here now. I ain't charming you, Mira. I'm speaking truth."

And he meant that. Demon Winter had done his fair share of wooing women. But no woman he had ever known had come close to this one. Mira was unparalleled. Everything he said to her emerged from a place of deep, abiding honesty. She made him feel things he had not known were possible. This passion between them would necessarily come to an end because of the differences in their worlds, but he never wanted her to doubt how lovely and desirable she was.

She kissed the pad of his thumb, a sensual smile curving her lips. "You are a dangerous man, Damian Winter. I like you far, far too much."

"Tell me something," he said, running his forefinger along her silken jaw as he studied the lustrous beauty of her face. "If you could be anywhere in this moment, with anyone, who would you choose to be with and where?"

"I would be Mira and Damian." Her soft voice curled around him like a caress. "I would not be anywhere else or with anyone else."

"Not if you could be free, truly free?" he pressed, for he had sensed she was unhappy with her circumstances. That she felt mired by obligation, even with her husband gone.

"I am as free as I am able to be when I am with you." There was a tinge of sadness underlying her words.

He kissed her, feeling that sadness burrow itself in his heart. When their lips parted, they were both breathless and beyond words. With Mira's help, Damian shucked his own garments until no more cloth barriers existed between them. She was positioned at an erotic angle on the pillows, her body like an offering he could not resist. He parted her folds, finding her slick with dew. Hot and ready.

Her hands traveled all over, anointing him with fire. *Yes*, he thought. *Touch me, Mira. Take what you want.* Or mayhap he spoke the words aloud. He was beyond knowing. As if she had heard him, she took his erect cock in a firm grasp and stroked him. More heat exploded, beginning in his cock, radiating out. His ballocks tightened. His hips thrust.

"Put me inside you," he told her.

She did, guiding him to her entrance. One thrust, and he

was deep in her welcoming warmth. She gripped him tight, so tight. They had spent many nights like this, wrapped up in each other, and each time was more potent than the last. He did not think he could ever get his fill of her.

Although he wanted to savor their joining, his body took complete command of his mind. He made love to her fast and hard, sliding in and out of her in a rhythm that had them both moaning and panting. He took a succulent, berry-pink nipple in his mouth and sucked as his fingers worked over her pearl. She arched into him, crying out, wild in her pleasure, her nails scoring his back.

Likely, she would leave marks. Mayhap draw blood. But he wanted it. He wanted her savagery, her intensity. He wanted her. Desperately. Everything she had to give and more.

Desire rolled down his spine as she clenched on him, crying out her pleasure in wild abandon. He shifted his position then, bringing him deeper, taking both her hands in his and lacing their fingers. Their palms perfectly aligned, Demon pinned her hands to the pillows on either side of her head. Again and again, he thrust. The slickness of her spend coated him. The scent of her perfumed the air, floral, exotic, and musky. Her breathy moans spurred him on as she wrapped her legs around his waist.

"Look at me, Mira," he urged as he hovered over her.

Her eyes fluttered open, the brilliance of her blue gaze hitting him anew. Her fingers tightened on his. This was more than a mere tupping. So much more. He had never felt the depth of connection he felt with Mira before. It was terrifying and yet it felt bloody good.

"Damian," she whispered, so much emotion in her voice. "I...*oh.*"

Her words trailed off, and he knew a moment of regret that she did not finish them. What had she been about to say?

He wanted those words, wanted her feverish surrender. But then the ripples of her climax—yet another—tightened on his shaft, and he was lost. She felt too good, clasping him, holding him as if inside her was where he belonged.

The ferocity of his orgasm was astounding, crashing over him like the storm-tossed waves of a sea. He did not have enough time to withdraw. Instead, he pumped into her, exploding, filling her with his seed as he sealed his lips to hers.

They kissed, hearts thundering in unison, as the world around them returned. Later, he would regret what he had done, the lack of care he had taken yet again when he had vowed not to do so after the first.

What the devil was the matter with him?

For now, he could not even give a damn. All he wanted was to revel in the miraculous feeling of this woman beneath him, her body pressed to his, their mouths moving together in sweet, slow splendor.

CHAPTER 7

Fucking hell.
 Sodding, fucking, floating hell.

In the grim quiet of his sister's office, Demon sat, staring unseeing at the ledgers before him. He had made a mistake. A grave mistake. A grim one, and he had not made it merely once, but twice.

It was the sort of mistake he had never, in all his eight-and-twenty years, made. The sort he had vowed to *never* allow, regardless of the reason, the woman, the moment. The sort that could land him in more trouble than Gen discovering he was fucking one of the fancy ladies who was a member of her gaming hell.

The sort that could make him a *father*.

Why the hell did the notion of claiming that particular title not horrify him as much as it should?

"Yournabs?"

He shook himself, running a hand along his jaw, and found Davy standing before him on the threshold. "Demon or Mr. Winter will do, lad. I ain't a cull and you know it."

"Right you are. The shipment of Madeira's come. Thought you wanted to 'ave a look."

They had been two bottles short last shipment. "Thank you, lad. You are correct."

He rose and skirted the desk.

"Not going to need the pen, are you?" Davy asked, eyeing him oddly.

Christ.

Demon glanced down, realizing he was still holding his quill, which was looking rather strangled at the moment. "Of course not."

Grimly, he thrust it into the well, cursing himself and Mira for the effect she had upon him. His mind was addled. Rotten. Mayhap she had placed a curse upon him. That was what this felt like—the all-consuming need for her, coupled with the frustration at his lack of control.

He had risen that morning to the scent of her on his sheets. She had been long gone, having been handed into her carriage by him some time after midnight. But the memories had lingered like the sweet floral fragrance. And despite the guilt twisting his guts over what he had done, he had taken himself in hand to the thought of her supple curves beneath him and the drenched heat of her cunny gripping his cock like a vise.

Once more caught up in his thoughts, Demon somehow managed to upend the inkwell on Gen's desk. A massive blot spread on the surface. His sister was going to blacken his eye.

"Christ," he muttered. "Davy, fetch something to clean this, will you?"

The scamp was already there, moving faster than Demon had anticipated, a cloth in hand as he righted the inkwell and mopped up the ink. "There you are, yournabs. No 'arm done. I'll see it cleaned, I will."

The scamp had been astonishingly helpful since his

return from his sojourn under Mira's protective wing. He had claimed he preferred to be at Lady Fortune. Indeed, he had not—at least to Demon's knowledge—thieved so much as a feather from a lady's hair. Moreover, he had proven himself something of a shadow. But a useful one.

Demon frowned at Davy, who had mopped up the ink and was frantically scrubbing before a lasting stain permeated the polish. "Lad, as I told you, I ain't a lord. Call me Demon or Mr. Winter or sir. No more *yournabs*, you hear?"

There was something about the pretensions of a lordly title which disturbed him. More so now that he was lusting after a woman who was beyond his reach. One who shared her body with him but did not deem him worthy of learning her full name. But there was also something deuced odd about Davy's sudden angelic behavior.

"Sorry, your—*sir.*" The lad continued scrubbing. "I'll see to this. You best go and check on the Madeira. Count 'em thrice."

Their wine merchant was an unscrupulous bastard. But he also sold the best wine for the best price. Even with missing bottles, Lady Fortune was well ahead of the game. However, it did not sit well with Demon that someone had been cheating them. The merchant claimed his deliveries were complete. No one had counted the last delivery. Which meant some bottles could well have been stolen.

Demon nodded, an unexpected feeling of tenderness toward the scamp rising within him, along with something else. Pride, odd as it seemed. "Thank you, Davy. I will return in a few minutes. No thieving whilst I'm gone."

Davy tugged at his forelock. "Wouldn't dream of it, sir."

The little thief was growing on him, much like a barnacle on a ship's hull. He felt almost...fatherly toward the lad. Fancy that. Bemused, Demon spun on his heel and quit the office, lest he become truly maudlin or start knocking over the bloody chairs in his distraction. It was his stupidity the night before which was making him mad, and that was plain to see.

Give him one beautiful flame-haired widow with a tight, drenched cunny, and all he could think of was her. And siring offspring. *Good fucking God.* He had to grab the reins whilst he maintained whatever shreds of sanity he possessed.

He was not a father. Not a husband. Not someone eligible or suitable. Not a lord. Not a nice man. Hell, often, he was not the best of brothers, and he loved his family more than he loved anything, even gaming, charming, and twisting the people around him until they were in the palm of his hand. And that was saying something. The only reason he was helping Gen run Lady Fortune was because he had hoped he might bed some of the ladies who came to spend all their pin money, and that was the truth.

Until one lady in particular.

But he would not remain in her thrall for long. Demon had no doubt. This was a temporary spell. Soon enough, they would both move on.

Damnation. Why did the notion make him so bloody sad?

Demon made his way through the dimly lit halls to the rear entrance of Lady Fortune where tradesmen made their deliveries. He thrust open the door, blinking at the surprisingly bright sunlight. That was the thing about gaming hells he had always admired—you never knew what time of day it was or what the world was like beyond the heavy curtains. Gaming hells were places of chance, wagering, games, and drink. Sometimes wenches as well.

The crates of Madeira were awaiting him, but Hugo, the merchant, was nowhere to be found. What the devil?

"Hugo?" he called, casting a glance around the alley.

He spied a pair of boots first, sticking out from beneath the merchant's cart. Then legs.

Alarm shot through him.

Pain thundered down upon his head.

The world went black.

* * *

"A CRASH SOUNDED. All the hounds began to bark, racing for the source of the interruption," Joanna read to the drawing room.

"What manner of crash was it?" Gideon demanded.

Mirabel sighed, and was about to remind her youngest son to hold his tongue whilst his sister was sharing the story she had been so dutifully penning, when Percy stepped in.

"Hush, Gid," he chided, quite stepping into the role of oldest sibling these days. "Joanna is reading, and you must allow her to have her turn."

Her mouth snapped closed. Before her was cruel evidence of how quickly her children were growing. No longer babes who needed her tender embraces or handkerchief to dry their tears. Indeed, there would be no more babes to hold in her arms. No more first steps or first words.

Why did the thought bring with it such a ludicrous pang of longing? She had three children she loved, and she now had her freedom as well. What more could she ask for?

Him.

But she would not think of Damian Winter now. Nor would she contemplate the risks she had taken when she had allowed him to spend within her. But two mistakes would not matter, surely? She would be more careful next time. She would make certain there could be no recriminations.

And she would be wiser. Though an unwanted voice reminded her that if she were truly wise, there would not *be* a next time.

"Do you not agree, Mama?"

Percy's voice cut through her frantic, troubled thoughts, making her jump in her seat. She jerked her attention back to her children, guilt searing her for being so beset by distraction. Her children deserved all her attention.

Mirabel sighed. "Yes, of course I agree. Gideon, you must not interrupt your sister."

"I was only wanting to know what sort of crash it was. She did not say." Gideon shrugged.

Percy rolled his eyes heavenward, as if exasperated. "Mayhap she was about to, before you began chirping like a sparrow with your endless litany of questions."

"I'm not a sparrow!" Gideon, forever sensitive about being the youngest, puffed up his chest. "Did you know the reed sparrow doesn't sing? What is a litany?"

"A repetition," Mirabel explained gently. "Your curiosity is commendable, Gideon, but it can be tiresome, particularly when you are not exhibiting good manners."

"Was it a clang, as in swords clashing? What if it was a lion roaring? Can lions eat people?" Gideon continued, undeterred.

Joanna huffed. "May I finish my story?"

"Lions can eat people, I suppose," Mirabel found herself answering.

That was what Gideon did—he asked questions. His little head was filled with them. He also interrupted and tended to forget his manners. Walters often despaired of him. He was unique, her Gideon. Sometimes Mirabel wondered where his inquisitive, stubborn nature had derived from.

Her youngest son gasped. "How would a lion eat a person?"

"Lions only eat lads who ask too many questions," Percy said, his face expressionless.

But once more, Gideon continued, "Do lions understand questions?"

"Yes," said Percy.

"No," Mirabel reassured him simultaneously. "You needn't worry about lions, my dear. You shall never meet one."

"But what if there is a lion in Joanna's story?" he wondered. "I shall have nightmares."

"There are no lions in my story, you ninny," Joanna exclaimed. "If you will only cease talking so I may finish?"

"Go on," Mirabel urged her daughter, offering her what she hoped was a calm, encouraging smile.

They spent afternoons together, taking turns sharing whatever it was they were most proud of at the moment, and Mirabel treasured this time. Yesterday had been Percy's turn, and he had delighted them all with his nearly flawless recitation of Latin. The day before had been Gideon's, and to no one's surprise, he had regaled them with a collection of worms he had rounded up from their small gardens, along with a selection of bird feathers.

Joanna continued her story. "A crash sounded. All the hounds began to bark, racing for the source of the interruption…"

The remainder of the tale concluded without further disturbance from Gideon, thank heavens. Mirabel embraced each of her children and sent them back to their lessons with their governess. Not one quarter hour later, a most unexpected caller arrived.

Young Master Davy stood on the threshold of her drawing room, his countenance ashen. "My Grace. Something terrible's 'appened to Mr. Winter. You've got to come with me."

All the lightness in her heart from spending time with her children sputtered and turned to darkness. "What can it be, Davy?"

"The piss prophet is seeing to 'im now." The lad's eyes were shining with unshed tears.

It was the fear on his small face that had her heart pounding as confusion set in over what he was speaking of. "Piss prophet, Davy?"

"Doctor," he elaborated. "The sort what looks at a man's piss to decide what ails 'im. Don't know if this one is the sort or not. Don't like 'im much."

Dear God.

"Why does Mr. Winter need a doctor?" she asked, heart pounding.

"Someone attacked 'im," Davy told her. "Left 'im in the streets, bleeding from the knowledge box."

Mirabel supposed it was the lad's upset that had sent him into frantic cant that was nearly impossible for her to translate. But she could glean enough from him to understand that Damian had been beaten about the head and was being tended to by a physician.

She hauled Davy into a motherly embrace, not caring if the lad thieved her earrings or anything else. "Take me to him, lad."

* * *

A voice reached him.

The voice of an angel.

It was *her*.

Mira, bringing him back from the abyss.

Fingers tightened on his, and he clasped them, though his head ached. His eyelids felt as if they had been stitched shut. But slowly, he blinked them open, needing to reassure himself he was where he thought he was. That he hadn't cocked up his toes. That the soft, reassuring voice and the velvet touch belonged to Mira.

Her beautiful face was there, hovering over him. Her

brow was furrowed, her lips pinched, countenance paler than fresh cream.

"Mira," he tried to say.

But his voice was hoarse. Scarcely there. His throat was dry and sore, as if he had been sleeping a drunkard's slumber.

"Damian!" Her soft exclamation wrapped around him like an embrace.

There was such hope in her voice, such relief.

It was almost as if she had been…worried about him.

She squeezed his fingers tighter, leaning over him and bringing with her the exotic scent he could not resist. He inhaled deeply, confusion reigning. What the hell had happened? Why did his head ache? Why was she fretting over him?

The questions were there, yet his tongue remained oddly sluggish. So, too, his mind. He was cork-brained and he didn't know the reason.

Her fingers swept over his brow, brushing hair from his forehead with such tenderness, a strange, new ache took up residence within him. A longing he had no right to feel. One which confused him more than his current state did.

"How are you feeling, darling?" she asked, voice soothing.

"Like the devil," he managed. "What the hell happened?"

She frowned. "Do you not recall?"

He closed his eyes, inhaling slowly. Flowers and Mira twined about him, calming. Delectable. "Whatever it was, must've been bad. My fucking skull hurts."

Damnation. She was a lady. He should watch his tongue.

"Apologies," he mumbled, raising a hand to his throbbing head, only to find it covered in cloth. "Christ. What is this?"

"A bandage." Lush lips still downturned, she took his fingers in hers and gently guided them away from his head. "You were attacked, Damian. From what Davy told me, there was a wine merchant who arrived and he was attacked as well, just before you reached him."

"Hugo." Remembrance hit him now. Slowly. Surely. Why the hell did his mind feel so strange? "The boots and legs."

Her expression grew more puzzled. "Boots and legs?"

"I saw them," he tried to explain. "Knew something was wrong. But then someone attempted to lamb me. Feels as if he succeeded."

"Lamb?"

"Beating," he added. "My head is cloudy."

"Laudanum, no doubt, combined with the blow."

She was still frowning.

He did not like it.

With his free hand, Demon traced the vee in her forehead, trying to smooth it. "Smile, my lady. I ain't dead yet."

Her grip on him intensified. "Was that meant to be a sally?"

His head throbbed some more. "No? Yes?"

Whatever answer would make her smile. He wanted lightness in her face. The radiance she ordinarily shone with.

"You must not make light of your welfare, Mr. Winter," she told him, sounding as prim as she had on the day he had first met her.

And he had gone back to being Mr. Winter, he noted.

"Have I offended you?"

"Good heavens, no. Why do you ask?"

"You are scowling, love."

"I am not scowling." She blinked furiously, and for the first time, he realized the reason for the unnatural brilliance in her eyes.

Tears rolled down her cheeks. She dashed them away.

"Now you are weeping," he observed.

"What am I meant to do? You gave me a terrible fright!"

Her voice was high, almost shrill.

He winced, for it did nothing to quell his raging megrim. "Believe me, it was not my intention to have my knowledge box bashed."

"Knowledge box," she repeated, almost to herself. "That is what Davy called it as well."

Davy. As sluggish as his brain was acting, Demon began to make sense of what had happened.

"The lad came to you?" he asked.

"Yes, and quite fortunately too. It would seem no one knew how to reach your partner, and the physician who was summoned to aid you was not nearly as knowledgeable as he might have been. He was spooning laudanum down your throat when I arrived."

That would explain her earlier words and the fog inhabiting his mind both. As well as his stumbling tongue. "You sent him away?"

"He was giving you too much laudanum," she said. "I did not like it. When my…husband was ill, his attending physician was too happy to force laudanum upon him. The doctor promised me it would lessen his pain. However, I noticed too much of the stuff dulled his mind, and the more of it he was given, the more he required. The end of his life was a terrible blend of suffering and confusion. After a time, he no longer recognized any of us. Not even his mistress, whom he apparently loved quite well."

She had just revealed much to him. But Demon's mind was still an addled jumble. Later, he would unravel all these words. Make sense of them. Make sense of her.

"I am sorry for what you experienced, Mira," he said softly, longing to comfort her although his own head ached.

What the devil had his attacker hit him with? A blacksmith's hammer?

She raised his hand to her lips for a reverent kiss. "I am sorry for what happened to *you*, Damian, and that is what concerns me most. My past is where it belongs. Did you see your assailant?"

He tried to recall, but whether from the blow or his distraction at the time, his memories were vague and indistinct. He had been thinking of Mira. Had exited through the customary rear portal where tradesmen gathered to deliver their wares. At Davy's appearance in his office, he had gone to count the Madeira shipment. But Hugo had already been lying in the alley upon his appearance.

That much he was certain of.

The rest…

The rest remained as murky as a rainy night.

Demon rubbed his jaw. "I saw no one. What of Hugo, the wine merchant?"

Mira stared, her countenance grim.

"Christ. Hugo's dead?" he asked, though he did not need to. His answer was there, etched upon her beautiful, expressive face.

"There was a knife in his back," she confirmed, lower lip trembling. "Some of his stores were stolen."

His head ached. The information she had just given him did nothing to help matters. But just now, he did not want to think. What he wanted—nay, needed—was the woman before him.

"You came here for me?" he probed.

"Of course. Why would I not?"

He had not expected her concern. No one had ever fretted over him, aside from his siblings. Certainly not any of the women he had bedded in the past. But how to answer her?

"Thank you," he said simply, which seemed the best response of all. Still, she was too far removed from him, sitting at his bedside as if he were an invalid.

Demon Winter was not—nor would he ever be—a damned invalid.

"You need not thank me." She was gracious and polite as ever, his fire-haired seductress.

What had he done before she had come into his world? He did not want to remember. Nor did he want to think about what would happen when she left it as she inevitably must.

"Come into bed with me," he invited, hungering for her warmth.

Her eyes went wide. "You are injured."

"Not to make love." He laughed before grimacing at the pain such a gesture caused him, sobering right quick. "I don't want to bed you, Mira. Hell, I *do* want to bed you. Just not in this moment with my napper hurting as it does. In this moment, I only want you near to me. I want to hold you. Touch you. Feel you against me."

He reached for her.

She took his hand, and though she was dressed in as fine a gown as he had ever seen on a lady, all proper and perfect, she crawled on the bed with him. Mira slid beneath the counterpane, aligning her body with his. And everything was right in his world. His woman had her arm about his waist, her head on his chest. He was enveloped in sultry floral perfume and something far more intoxicating. Her care and concern.

She was too good for him.

But he was not too proud to bask in her whilst he could.

Hell, if taking a knock to the old nob was all it required for her to storm to his side, he would willingly accept the blow again, just to have her here, warm and tender and soft and wonderful, wrapped around him.

"Why do you think someone would try to do you harm, Damian?" she asked softly.

Ah, his sweet siren. She could not simply enjoy the closeness. She had to worry.

"Likely, the villain was after Hugo. You needn't concern yourself with my affairs." He pressed a kiss to her crown, inhaling deeply of her scent as he did so.

Floating hell, he was enamored of this woman. Even in pain as he was, his prick was beginning to rise. That was how strongly she affected him.

"How can you know he was after someone other than yourself?" she asked, her palm gliding over his chest in slow, reassuring motions. "Does this sort of thing happen often in your world?"

"It may," he allowed, thinking of the vast difference between the rookeries and the life to which she was accustomed.

She was a lady, living in the fashionable West End. She had been born to wealth, privilege, and the strictly guarded circles of her social set. Whilst he had been born a bastard in the East End, struggling from his first breath to now. The bond he had forged with his Winter siblings had granted him some measure of safety over time. Together, they had built a formidable presence. Many feared them. Others envied them and coveted what they had built.

It was the way of the world. He was not afraid to face whatever approached him. Or, as it were, snuck up behind him and beat him over the head.

Mira stiffened against him, her breath falling hot on his neck. "You are in danger, Damian. I do not like it."

"Here now, I ain't in danger." Though perhaps that was untrue, and the insistent ache in his head reminded him of that. So, too, the troublesome thought of Hugo's boots.

Hugo's murder.

Hell.

"You are lying to me."

Aye, he was. But if he was in danger, it was not her affair. There was no way a Mayfair lady could help him. He would take care from this moment on, lest whoever had killed Hugo and attacked him would return.

"I'll have a talk with the charleys about it." He nuzzled the fragrant copper curls bound in a tidy knot, wishing they would come undone so he could fan her locks over his pillow and run his fingers through them. "Do not trouble yourself over me. All my cards are trumps."

But as he lay there with Mira's soft, sweet warmth pressed against him, his head aching, he could not deny the lingering fear curdling his gut. The fear not just that an unknown foe was after him, waiting to strike again, but that his time with Mira would soon have to come to an end.

CHAPTER 8

Mira woke, disoriented. And wrapped in man.

Delicious, handsome, warm, seductive man.

Damian Winter, to be precise.

His dark gaze was on her through the low morning light filtering past the window dressing. She fell into that impenetrable stare, mesmerized, until she realized she had spent the night—the entire night—in his bed.

She had never returned home.

She shot into a seated position, guilt lancing her. "I must go."

"Must you?" His voice was a low, haunting rumble that threatened to lure her back to his side.

"Yes." She was wearing nothing but her chemise, which she had stripped to at some point in the evening. "Good heavens, I am going to have to return home in the same gown I left in yesterday."

What would her children think?

What would her servants think?

This was the sort of scandal she could not afford to

create. One wrong whisper could taint her reputation. Could ruin everything she had worked so hard to cultivate all these years for her children's sake.

"I will have Davy fetch you a gown," he suggested with a calm she wished she felt.

But this was urgent. She could not appear at Tarlington House dressed as she had been when she left. Moreover, her children and Octavia were surely wondering where she had gone. Although she had told her sister where she was headed and the necessity of her sudden departure, she had not intended to stay the whole night.

She glanced at him, finding him watching her from where he lay propped upon his pillows. The bandage on his head had been removed, and his mahogany hair was rakishly tousled, the gash he had suffered hidden by the thick waves. A shadow of whiskers shaded his jaw. He was alarmingly handsome.

And tempting.

She wetted her suddenly dry lips and gave in to curiosity. "Where would Davy find a gown?"

Had one of his paramours left her garments behind? The thought had her tensing more than she already was. It occurred to her suddenly how little she knew of this man she had spent the night with. This man to whom she had given her body.

"My sister," he said, dispelling her concerns with ease.

"Oh."

"I do not make a habit of keeping gowns of former lovers strewn about." He grinned, then rubbed his head. "Christ, that hurts. When I find the bastard responsible, I've got something in mind for him."

His words took her back to the danger surrounding him.

She frowned. "You are fortunate you are only suffering

from an aching head this morning, Damian. It could have been worse. Far worse. You could have been…"

Her voice broke. She could not allow herself to finish the horrendous, terrifying thought. Mirabel did not know when or how, but this man had stormed past her defenses. He inspired a tenderness within her that she had never felt for any man.

And after such a short amount of time.

Pity he was too young.

And the owner of a gaming hell.

And a beautiful sinner who lived in the East End.

"We've been through this, love." He reached for her, catching her around the waist and hauling her back to him. "You needn't fret over me. I'm a Winter. We always land on our feet when we fall out of windows."

She found herself clinging to him, absorbing his strength and vitality rather than withdrawing and rushing home as she had intended. The bed smelled like him. And he was rakish and charming and everything she should not want.

"How many windows have you fallen from?" she dared to ask.

"None." He leaned forward and kissed the tip of her nose. "You are beautiful in the morning."

She was sure she was not, but his words warmed her nonetheless. "You are trying to distract me."

"I am telling you the truth." He took her mouth then in a slow, soft kiss that left her breathless and clinging to him before he ended it. "And trying to distract you. Is it working?"

Dear God, yes. His nearness was working. His lips were working. His gentle touches were working. This man could cast a spell upon her without trying, and she knew it. She had let him.

He is dangerous, whispered the voice of reason.

The one she promptly silenced.

"Is your head feeling any better this morning?" she asked, worrying about the blow he had received, which had been enough to require some stitches.

"Much better with you here," he said, his grin fading. "Thank you for running to my rescue last night."

"Davy was quite convincing," she said, heat rising in her cheeks. "And I hardly rescued you. You were already safe when I arrived, thank heavens."

She had been terrified on Damian's behalf as well, but that was neither here nor there. Her relief at seeing him, alive if not well, had turned her knees to jam. She had sunk into the nearest chair at his bedside, overwhelmed.

He cupped her cheek, caressing her with so much tenderness, her heart gave a pang. "It is a habit of yours, is it not?"

"What is a habit?" She studied his brown eyes, noticing the glints of cinnamon and gold, the dark circle ringing the iris.

His eyes were lovely. Far too lovely for a man. His lashes, too, were long. His cheekbones high. His lips surprisingly full. It was as if he had been fashioned as an homage to masculine magnificence.

"Worrying over everyone save yourself," he elaborated softly. "I have not known you for long, Mira, but I have seen the way you care for those around you. Davy, your children, your sister. Hell, you fret over me, and I am certainly not worthy of your concerns."

"Of course you are," she was quick to counter.

Because it was true. She had seen enough of him to know he was a good man, a kind man, gentle-hearted and true. Though he may run a gaming hell and live in the East End, and though he had been born on the wrong side of the blanket, he was so much more than his circumstances. He had been caring and worshipful with her. His compassion for the hungry had him making certain they were fed each night. He was patient with Davy, and the lad watched him with undisguised adoration. During the course of their frantic carriage ride to Lady Fortune the night before, Davy had revealed to her that he considered Demon Winter an honorary father of sorts.

On account of us being so similar and all, Davy had added, rubbing the back of his hand over his running nose and tearful eyes until Mirabel had gently chastised him and he had withdrawn a dirt-smudged handkerchief instead.

"I ain't." Damian shook his head, then winced. "Fuck me, I forgot about my noodle." He paused, then winced again. "Christ. Not watching my tongue properly, am I? Blame it on the knock to my head?"

"I am sorry." It pained her to see him hurting. "Shall I fetch you something? Laudanum? A poultice?"

"You, Mira. You're all I need." He pressed his forehead to hers, his warm breath coasting over her lips in the tantalizing prelude to a kiss.

He needed her? Strange to think it, but she needed him as well.

This connection they shared, this bond they had forged, it went beyond the physicality of their joining. She felt things for him. Things she had never felt before for another man.

Things which terrified her.

But still, she could not resist settling her hands on his shoulders and turning her face up, seeking his kiss. He did not disappoint her. His mouth moved over hers, knowing what she wanted. What she needed.

Lulling her into the fantasy she could remain here in bed with him forever.

That was not to be, however. Percy, Joanna, and Gideon needed her. So, too, Octavia. To say nothing of the potential repercussions which would be caused by her absence.

Heavens, she had never dismissed her coachman. He must have spent the evening in the mews. She would triple his earnings to make amends and ensure his silence.

She tore her lips from Damian's, breathless. "I must go. My children will wonder where I am."

"I am selfish and I want to keep you here, to myself." He kissed her again, swiftly, lingeringly, before kissing the tip of her nose once more. "But your children must come first, Mira. I understand."

He did, she knew.

And somehow, that made her heart ache more as she took her reluctant leave of him.

* * *

"As close as God's curse to a whore's arse."

Mirabel blinked at her sister. "Surely you did not say what I think you did."

Octavia was an original. She was free in her speech and thought, and she had never fit the mold society would have forced her into. However, Mirabel was still reasonably certain she must have misheard Octavia.

Her sister repeated herself, verbatim.

Mirabel felt weak. "And Gideon said this?"

Octavia was grim. "To his governess, no less. Apparently, she was standing too near to him when he was attempting to recite his French."

"Where would he have possibly heard such a phrase, do you suppose?" she asked, though she feared she knew.

And that he was a golden-haired rascal who referred to her as *My Grace* and could not seem to help himself from thieving anything in his vicinity. Although, to his credit, she had not noticed a thing missing from her person or reticule this morning, much to her delight and relief.

"Your Young Master Davy, of course," Octavia answered needlessly. "Gideon admitted so to the governess after she boxed his ears."

Mirabel's body went hot. She was incredibly protective of her children. No one was permitted to punish them without her approval, and Walters was aware of this rule.

"She boxed his ears?" Mirabel repeated.

Her sister's countenance grew worried. "I knew you would be displeased when Percy told me what had happened. Gideon was crying, and Joanna was doing her utmost to comfort him. The uproar led me to the schoolroom."

Her son had been physically hurt. *Punished.* He had been crying.

And where had Mirabel been? Kissing a man who was ten years her junior in the East End after he had been set upon by a footpad and she had spent the night in his bed.

Shame warred with outrage for precedence.

Her heart was breaking.

"Mirabel?"

Octavia's concerned voice cut through her riotous thoughts. She attempted to take a deep breath, but her chest hurt. Her eyes were stinging with tears of her own. "I should have been here."

"I was here," her sister reassured her. "I am sorry I was not able to stop what happened with the governess. Had I been aware there was an issue, I would have intervened sooner."

"No," she managed, attempting to gather her wildly vacillating emotions before continuing. "You have nothing for which you need apologize, Octavia. You are an excellent auntie and sister. I, however... I have failed my children."

Just as Stanhope had always expected her to.

"You did not fail them," Octavia hastened to argue. "For the first time in your life, you are living for yourself, and not just for your children and husband. Stanhope was a terrible man, and you know it. There is no harm in seeking that which makes you happy."

She swallowed. "There is when it affects my children."

Mirabel closed her eyes and inhaled, the world swirling and swimming about her. When she had been younger, she had fallen into the lake at their country estate in Staffordshire when she had made the foolish mistake of attempting to reach a feather which had blown from her hat. She had been unable to swim. The lake had been deep, the waters over her head. She still recalled frantically flapping her arms and legs, the tangle of her skirts and petticoats about her legs. The terror of thinking herself lost.

Until her groomsman had plucked her from the water, coughing and sputtering and terrified. But alive.

She felt that same strange frenzy of fear now, the certain knowledge that one wrong move would prove her end.

"Mirabel."

Octavia's voice reached her, permeating the roaring in her ears. Cutting through those dark memories. Her eyes opened to find her sister staring at her with a concerned expression on her face.

"I need to see Walters now," she managed.

She was going to sack the woman. There was no question. Her rules were clear, and she made no exceptions. Not when it came to her beloved children.

"There can be no harm in searching for some small measure of comfort," Octavia pressed. "It is nothing less than you deserve. Indeed, it is what you have *always* deserved. Stanhope was a heartless arse."

"He was a duke." It was hardly a defense, and Mirabel knew it. Moreover, the argument was one her own mother had wielded against her often during her contentious marriage to Stanhope.

Unhappiness had not perturbed Mama. Nor had abuse. Lack of an excellent marriage, however, did. Which was why she had been more than pleased to cast Octavia off upon Mirabel.

"Dukes are arses as well as untitled gentlemen," her sister countered.

And she was not wrong, curse her. Octavia had always been wise beyond her years. It was likely why she had never married herself. There had been many days when Mirabel had wished she herself had not. But her children had rendered her every sacrifice and misery as Stanhope's wife worthwhile.

"I should not have gone running to him yesterday," Mirabel said anyway, more guilt making her stomach knot. "If I had not gone, I would have been here. Indeed, if I had not gone there, and if I had not insisted upon bringing Davy here, Gideon never would have heard such vulgar language. Nor would he have repeated it. This entire situation could have been avoided if I had only been content to be proper and circumspect and to do my duty."

"Now you sound like our mother," Octavia accused, frowning mightily. "I wholeheartedly disapprove. There is nothing wrong with seeking happiness, Mirabel. The only thing which is truly wrong is believing yourself unworthy of it."

"I am not worthy of it when it is detrimental to my children." Tears were pricking her eyes. She blinked them away. "This is just as I feared. A terrible mistake."

"Mirabel—"

"No," she interrupted her sister sternly. "It is true. I have made a dreadful muddle of things, and I must rectify it."

But first, she needed to remove Walters from her position and find a suitable replacement.

CHAPTER 9

The evening rush would come soon enough to Lady Fortune, and Demon had no end of problems facing him, none of which were aided one whit by the aching in his skull. Hugo's murderer had cracked him over the crown with something deuced vicious. All things considered, he was lucky to be alive. The memory of the wine merchant's body sprawled in the alley would forever haunt him.

Hugo was not a friend or acquaintance, but he was someone Demon had dealt with at regular intervals. And to think he would be no more…to think of the violence which had beset him prior to his end…

A shiver went down Demon's spine.

Seated at the desk in his sister's office, Demon dropped his head to his hands, rubbing his temples. His inquiries with the charleys, who were in his brother Dom's pay, had led him nowhere. Hugo had paid his creditors. There did not appear to be any customers in turn who owed him enough funds to answer them with murder. Nor had there been any word of the previous day's proceedings in any of the usual haunts. Everyone was silent. No one had seen what had happened to

Demon or the wine merchant. If Davy had not come looking for him when he had, Demon might have cocked up his toes as well.

But more than the mystery of what the hell had happened the day before—and why—Demon was haunted by one thing. One person.

Mira.

She had spent the night in his bed. For the first time, he had risen with a woman in his arms. And he had liked it far, far too much. Had liked it enough to risk another ferocious blow to the head if it meant the chance for one more such night.

"Christ," he muttered to himself. "I didn't even fuck her."

"You didn't fuck 'er?"

At the sound of the familiar voice, Demon's head shot up, sending more pain slicing through him. The door to Gen's office stood open without his having heard it. Davy was on the threshold, hair disheveled, rascal's grin on his lips.

"Here now, scamp." He frowned, which required more effort than his aching head appreciated at the moment. "You aren't to repeat such words. Am I understood?"

"If I ain't to say 'em, why does you?" Davy countered, grinning and revealing his missing top tooth.

"Why *do* you?" Demon corrected grimly, knowing he should teach the lad better.

Hell, if Davy ever wanted to make more of himself than a pickpocket, he would *need* to know better.

"Don't know, yournabs. Cause you prefers 'em?" Davy shrugged.

"No, Davy. That is not what I was asking. I was attempting to show you the correct way to ask your question." He sighed. "The proper way to say it is as follows, lad. Listen closely. If I am not to say them, then why do you?"

Davy grinned. "But I just 'eard you say 'em."

WINTER'S WIDOW

Something occurred to Demon then, above the thumping in his aching head. "Are you bamboozling me, scamp?"

"Why would I bumfuzzle you, yournabs?"

He laughed. Which hurt. So he winced and held his aching head. "Christ, Davy. The correct word is *bamboozle*. Do me a favor, eh? Do not go about saying *bumfuzzle*. It sounds…hell…never mind."

The lad tugged on his forelock. "Aye, yournabs."

"What was it you came here for, Davy?" he asked, because half of him was certain the lad had appeared with the sole purpose of vexing him and playing his games.

"I was worried about you." Davy hung his head, kicking his scuffed boots on the carpets. "Not every day you almost kick the bucket."

As if Demon required the reminder. "I appreciate your concern, but I ain't dead yet, as you can see. Anything else, Davy?"

"New Pup shat on the floor again, sir," the lad announced.

"Damnation," he ground out. "Where?"

"Kitchens," Davy replied, as if in song.

"Are you bloody *singing*?" he demanded, feeling cantankerous as a bull.

Davy blinked. "No, yournabs. Mayhap a bit, on account of you not being a dustman and all."

"Stop calling me yournabs," he commanded. "I ain't a lord. And I ain't dead yet, so you can stop referring to what happened yesterday. I was at the wrong place at the wrong time, but I am here. That is all that need concern you now."

And never had he been more aware of the fact that he was not a lord than during the time he had spent with Mira. To be called *yournabs* now held a different meaning than it once had done. Because it had become a ceaseless reminder of what he was not and what he could never be. A reminder that whilst she cared enough to spend the night with him, she had left in haste by the morning light and she had failed to appear or send word in all the hours since.

But what had he expected from her? A proposal of marriage? *Mother of all saints*, the blow he had taken to the head had addled his wits more than he had realized. It had rendered him fucking *maudlin*.

Demon did not like it.

"Apologies, sir," Davy said, cutting through his thoughts once more. "Thought you'd want to know Chef is threatening to leave if we can't get New Pup to stop the grubshite in 'is kitchens."

"I told you, lad, his name isn't New Pup."

The feminine voice carrying from the hall was unmistakably Demon's half sister, Genevieve, the new Marchioness of Sundenbury. She breezed over the threshold, clad in her customary trousers, coat, and cravat, looking nothing like the fine lady she had become.

The one who was fooling all polite London as she took it by storm.

Demon shot to his feet out of respect for his beloved sibling before casting a glare at Davy. "Go on and clean up after the pup, lad. Tell chef New Pup will be kept from the kitchens until he learns to behave."

"His name is Lancelot," Gen groused.

"Fancy name for a fancy lady," Davy and Demon said at once.

Hell.

It was as if the lad were a reflection of himself at a younger age. Demon had seen it before. It was one of the reasons why he held the lad to such high standards and punished him thoroughly when he was in need of correction. But never so clearly as this moment.

They stared at each other, both bemused.

"Here now," Gen said, chuckling. "Are you sure Davy isn't your whelp?"

Not a chance of that. He had only spent his seed inside one woman to whom he was not wed. *Hell.* That was hardly a matter of pride, was it?

"I take care when I am with a woman," he growled, hating himself for the lie. Although, in fairness, he always *had* taken exacting care. Until Mira. "Not that this is a topic of discussion for a lady."

"Good thing I ain't a lady."

But Gen *was* a lady now, and Demon and Gen both knew it, even if Davy and the rest of the people in their employ were not privy to her secret. There was a difference in her. Not just that she had fallen in love with her husband the marquess—that was plain enough to see, and almost all Demon's half siblings had already fallen prey to the parson's mousetrap. Nothing new there. But what was new about Gen was the way she carried herself. There was a softness there which was new, a nod to elegance, which had been absent before. She was devoted to Sundenbury. Hopelessly in love.

Sickening was what it was.

"Good thing," Demon drawled, raising a brow before turning his attention to Davy. "Scatter, lad. Clean up the shite. Off you go."

Davy tugged at his forelock before disappearing, leaving Gen and Demon alone. Gen bent, tucking her fingers into her boot.

"The little bugger didn't try to steal my blade," she mused, sounding shocked.

Demon inclined his head. "The lad is changing his ways."

Her eyes narrowed. "Why now?'

She was right to question it.

He had not shared the incident concerning Mira and Davy—the theft of the ring, the subsequent departure of

Davy, followed by his abrupt return. The reasons for omitting it were obvious. He did not want to discuss Mira. Or receive a tongue lashing from his sister.

Demon rubbed his jaw. "No reason."

"Do not lie to me," she persisted. "Lie to others. Not me."

He sighed. "There was an incident. Davy thieved the ring of one of the ladies whilst helping her with her wrap. I have seen the matter settled. You needn't worry over it."

But had he seen the matter settled?

It hardly seemed so.

And *he* felt everything but settled.

"You are certain it has been taken care of?" Gen asked, frowning.

Although she was a married woman, the realities of which necessitated her living in Mayfair with her husband Lord Sundenbury, she was still quite involved in the operations of Lady Fortune. She had built the ladies' gaming hell from nothing with her own determination and resilience.

"Certain." He skirted the desk, thinking he must tell her about what had happened yesterday. She would do far worse than blacken his eye when she discovered he had gone to their brother Dom with the news first and that she had gone uninformed as the owner of Lady Fortune. Best to get her a bit soused first, he reasoned. "A flash of lightning for you, darling sister?"

"No drops of jackey for me today," she declined his offer of gin demurely, pressing a hand to her midriff. "Stomach's unsettled these days."

"Gen," he said, suspecting what she meant and forgetting all about the attack the day before for a moment.

She nodded. "Aye. 'Tis true. You'll be an uncle again soon."

"Fuck." The oath fled him. Seemed he was making a habit of the vulgar tongue today.

But if ever there was a time for losing control, it was now, when he had recently come upon the scene of a murder and he had been beaten over the head himself, only to have Gen announce she was going to be a mother.

Gen.

She was his baby sister. The one he and his brothers had looked after, fretted over, the one for whom they would wage war to defend her honor, much as they had done with that no-account Gregory she'd fancied herself in love with so long ago.

A small smile turned up her lips. "I was hoping you might be happy for us."

"Floating hell." He raked his fingers through his hair, forgetting himself. He winced and barely strangled his cry of pain as he glanced over his wound. "*Damn.* I am. Of course, I am. But you are still scarcely more than a babe to me. I am shocked, is all. Felicitations to you and the marquess. What does the duke make of your news?"

The Duke of Linross was her husband's father, who had not been keen on any of his aristocratic children marrying into the Winter clan. And almost every one of his children had, save the eldest daughter.

"He possesses the manners of an ill-tempered goat," Gen declared. "He'll not be happy unless it's a son and heir, and even then, he'll wish it were a proper lady whelping the lad instead of me. Is something wrong with you? You were wincing just now."

"Has he attempted to eat your shoe?" he tried to joke, although he was filled with inner rage on her behalf. The Duke of Linross was a pompous arse, as were most of the quality.

Demon was also carefully ignoring her query.

Gen's eyes narrowed. "You are trying to distract me. What happened to your head?"

Damn it. He should have known better than to think he

could keep what had happened to him from her. Gen was stubborn and determined in a way few others were. If she did not have her answer from him, she would interrogate every person in her employ until she discovered what had occurred. Her persistence did not bode well for keeping his secret.

"There was an incident," he began.

Her eyebrows rose. "Bloody hell, Demon. Not another incident. What was it, when did it happen, and why has no one told me?"

"Yesterday. The wine merchant, Hugo, was attacked in the alley." He paused, considering how he might best relay the information without causing his sister to worry too much. In her delicate condition, she needed to be calm. "I had the misfortune to interrupt the bastard, and he clubbed me over the head for my efforts. And no one told you because I am taking care of the matter. You needn't worry over it, especially now that I know you're having a babe."

She was, predictably, furious at his response. "You cannot decide what I am told, damn your hide. This is my bloody hell, unless you have forgotten."

"Of course I haven't forgotten, but neither have I forgotten that we need to keep your identity a secret. You cannot go sticking your nose in this one, Gen. You're married to Sundenbury now. I know what you're thinking, and I wasn't keeping this from you because you are my younger sister. The entire affair was a mistake, and the further you are from anything dangerous, the better."

Everything he had just said was the truth. But he also should have known better.

Gen tensed, her shoulders drawing back as if she were facing whoever had been responsible for the attack instead of standing in the safety of her office. "That's utter shite and you know it. What are we going to do about this? It cannot go unanswered. We will hunt down the villain who did this and see him arrested."

He could not help but to note that his sister sounded, for all her outrage, quite ladylike in her response, aside from her oath. She had changed much these past few months, and when she became a mother, she would further change, he had no doubt.

Good thing he was not settling down himself. He never wanted to change. Or at least, he had not believed he wanted to. Where the hell were these strange new feelings of longing emerging from?

He tamped them down.

"I've already spoken with Dom and the charleys," he reassured her. "We will find whoever did it. A doctor stitched my head up, and I have lived to see another day. For now, all we can do is wait. And find another wine merchant."

Gen studied him, her countenance grim. "It could have been worse, Demon. You could have been killed yourself."

The reminder sent a shiver down his spine, but he ignored it. "I wasn't. I'm here to run your hell. All is well."

"I don't like it. If something happens when I am not here, send word to me. Come to me first, not Dom. I'll see that we increase our guards in the mews and alley. This cannot happen again, not just because you are my brother and I love you, but because if word of such an attack were to reach the ladies who attend, they would cease coming here."

He clenched his jaw. "No one knows."

With the exception of *number one hundred four*.

Christ. He had all but forgotten that Mira was a club patron. Over the time they had spent together, she had become so much more. Too much more. Far more than he should have allowed.

"What is it you need to tell me, Demon?" Gen demanded,

having long ago been blessed with the ability to read her brothers' guilty faces.

"There is one member who is aware of what happened," he allowed reluctantly, preparing himself for his sister's fury.

Instead, she cocked her head, studying him. "Damn it, Demon. Have you been making the beast with two backs with one of our ladies?"

His cheeks went hot, his cravat instantly too tight. He slid a finger into the knot in an effort to loosen it. "Where did you learn such coarse language?"

"From you, arsehole."

Right. So she had. Even his ears were aflame. He had no defense. None. So he decided to deflect the blame.

"Hardly the speech of a future duchess, sister."

"I ain't a duchess yet, brother." Her chin went up. "You know the rule, Demon. You had but one."

Fuck. She was not wrong.

"She is…" He struggled to describe Mira to Gen, to make her understand why he had been driven to sever his one and only rule at Lady Fortune. *No bedding the ladies.* "Mira is not like the others. She is kindhearted and beautiful and all that is good and sweet. She is a widow with three children, and she tells them a story every day before they go to bed. She tended to me last night when I was injured. Spent the night here at great peril to her own reputation. She is trustworthy and loyal. This I know because of the mother she is. Because of how thoroughly she has trusted me, when she likely should not…"

Demon allowed his words to trail away as he belatedly took note of the expression on Gen's face.

"What, curse you?" he demanded, tugging once more on his cravat. *Stupid bloody knot.*

"I never thought I'd see it." She shook her head, her voice tinged with awe.

He glared at her, although it hurt his damned head to do so. "Never thought you'd see what, Gen?"

"Demon Winter in love." She grinned. "You love this woman, this Mira of yours."

Her words were akin to a pail of ice water being dumped over his head. "I do not."

Love was...impossible, weak, wrong, ludicrous, foolish.

Love was an illusion. A game.

And if he had fallen prey to it, he would certainly never be stupid enough to lose his heart to a woman who was so woefully beyond his reach that there was no possibility of ever making her truly his.

"She is not mine."

Nor would she ever be. *By God*, she did not entrust him with her own name. She would never give him herself. Not truly, not in any way beyond the physicality of their union. She offered him her body, but nothing more.

"You want her to be yours," Gen said softly.

And damnation, maybe the blow he had taken to his head the day before had rattled his brains loose, because here and now, as he stood before his sister, realization hit him square in the gut.

He did want Mira to be his. Forever.

Mother of all saints.

"I ain't in love with her," he muttered.

But as he issued the denial, he knew the words for a lie.

* * *

Mira had vowed she was not going to return to Lady Fortune.

After sacking the governess, arranging inquiries for a replacement, and commiserating with her children—whilst sternly reprimanding Gideon for his vulgar choice of words

—she had sat alone for some time, writing in her journal. It had become a habit of hers during the beginning of her marriage to Stanhope, a means of pouring all her misery into words and thus rendering the unhappiness of her marriage somehow bearable. Without her sister's company and the lively squabbling of her children, Mira had made a realization.

She was not ready to sever ties with Damian Winter so abruptly. Her heart, her body, *everything* within her called for one more night. In her journal, she crafted a list of reasons why she could not simply end her affair without seeing him again. He had been injured. She was still fretting over his condition. She needed the chance to say a proper farewell. Their time together had been too brief. She was not yet ready for it to end.

And so, her decision had been made. Just as she had every evening for the last fortnight, she readied herself for a trip to Lady Fortune. This time, she had taken additional care with her toilette. Her lady's maid had spent extra time on her hair, fashioning ringlets which framed her face. Her gown was a deep shade of blue to complement her eyes, because Damian had once said her eyes were his favorite color.

She had arrived at the private entrance to Lady Fortune and had been instantly shepherded to Damian's apartments. She had awaited him there, tense and uncertain. But then, he had opened the door and crossed the threshold, more handsome than any man ought to be, and he had looked at her as if she were the most glorious woman he had ever beheld.

All her misgivings had fled. They had wound up in a tangle on his bed, equally eager for each other. And she had gotten her wish. One more night in his arms. One more night of his kisses and caresses. One more night of surrendering to sin.

The trouble was, it hardly felt like sin now when she was

wrapped in his heat and strength, naked with him beneath the bedclothes, watching him sleep. In slumber, his face was smooth, almost angelic.

Her fingers itched to stroke the lock of hair that had fallen over his brow, just as her lips burned to kiss his. But she was hesitant to wake him. Reluctant to end this moment of peace. Because all too soon she would leave him, and this time, she would not return.

In the frenzy of their lovemaking, she had found neither the mental clarity nor the opportunity to speak to him about putting an end to their arrangement. And as she lay surrounded by his warmth, his scent curled around her, the haven of his bed a paradise she could not bear to leave, Mirabel did not think she could.

Her heart ached at the notion of never seeing him again, never knowing his touch, his kiss, the feeling of him deep inside her. Tears rose, stinging her eyes, but she bit her lip, sending them away, tamping down the emotion. Her years as the Duchess of Stanhope had taught her all too well how to harden herself. How to pretend she did not care.

Instead, she stroked his hair. Softly at first, hesitantly, lest she wake him up. Then with greater confidence, enjoying the texture of the tousled mahogany waves beneath her fingers.

"Mmm." He inhaled deeply, then sighed, his eyes opening to reveal a surprisingly alert gaze.

"Scoundrel." Although her tone was soft and teasing, taking the sting from her accusation, she pulled back her hand as if it had been seared, embarrassed to have been caught caressing him outside the act of lovemaking. That was what their relationship had been built upon—their mutual desire—had it not? "I thought you were asleep."

He gave her a rakish grin. "If you will promise to continue petting me, I will happily feign sleep."

A startled peal of laughter tore from her, welcome after the weightiness of her thoughts. "I was not petting you."

"Whatever you wish to call it, love." He punctuated the teasing in his tone with a wink. "I liked it."

Her heart beat faster, seemingly tripping over itself.

This man.

This wonderful, witty, handsome, sinful, delectable, caring, delicious, forbidden man. How could she ever say goodbye to him? How could she leave him tonight and never see him again? It seemed an impossibility. A betrayal of the worst order. But she must not think of that now.

"If you liked it," she said slowly, sending him a wicked grin of her own, "then I have no choice but to continue. Have I?"

She ran her fingers through his hair once more.

"No choice at all," he affirmed, shifting his head on the pillow so he could study her more fully.

"How is your head?" she asked, realizing far too late that she had not inquired after his welfare. She had been so caught up in the sight of him, vital and potent and masculine striding over the threshold to take her in his arms and make her mindless with his kisses, that she had not thought to ask until now. "Forgive me for not asking sooner."

"It is perfect now that I have you here with me." His arms tightened around her waist, anchoring her to him more firmly. "Why are you so serious tonight, Mira?"

Curse him for being so dratted observant.

She had hoped she was not allowing the malaise within her to show.

"You were attacked," she said, which was certainly part of her solemnity, if not all.

"But I lived to see another day. I'll not have it concerning you. What happened was an accident, nothing more. I was at the wrong place at the wrong time. The charleys say someone had a vendetta against the wine merchant, and that is all."

The furrow between his brows suggested he was not being entirely truthful to her. Even his voice held a tinge of worry. But Mirabel could hardly blame him. There was much she had kept from him. Not just her identity, but also her intention that this night would be their last. Looking at him now—the earnestness of his gaze, the open concern and caring in his countenance—she did not think she could reveal the latter to him.

It would hurt too much.

And he would tempt her too much.

She would give in.

For the moment, she allowed her fingertip to trail over the divot in his otherwise smooth forehead. "You are certain that is all it was?"

She hated the thought of anything ill befalling him. Hated, too, the thought that she would no longer know if it did. After this evening, she would be relinquishing her membership at Lady Fortune. She would return to living the life of the circumspect widow. No matter how much the prospect left her feeling cold and unhappy.

"Certain. You needn't worry yourself, love." He kissed the tip of her nose. "What has put the shadows in your eyes?"

Tell him, urged the voice within.

She could not. He was so near. So earnest. So...

Dear heavens.

So *beloved*.

But that could not be, could it? She could not have fallen in love with Damian Winter, the least suitable man in London, one born on the wrong side of the blanket, the owner of a gaming hell, unrepentant rogue who had offered to be her lover...

She swallowed. "I am reluctant to leave you."

Mirabel could scarcely believe she had said it. And though she knew quite well he would assume she meant for the evening, the words were no less true. She was a coward, it seemed. A coward who was falling in love with him. A coward who was about to leave him.

"Then stay," he said, pressing a kiss to her cheek, her ear, her jaw. "Stay as long as you like, Mira. Stay forever."

Such a tempting invitation. The most tempting invitation she had ever received, in fact.

"I wish I could." Mirabel cupped his cheek, savoring their closeness, tucking these moments into her heart so she could remember them. She loved the dark prickle of whiskers on his sharp jaw and his warmth. "How I wish I could."

He turned his head on the pillow, pressing a kiss to the center of her palm. "But you have your children. They would miss their mother, I expect."

"I would miss them as well."

"Will you tell me about them?"

His request took her by surprise and made the ice her previous husband had cast around her heart melt further. "What would you like to know?"

"Anything you want to tell me. They are a part of you, Mira. I find myself longing to know everything there is to know about every part of you." He smiled tenderly, then caught her hand in his and pressed a kiss to the tips of her fingers, stroking them with his thumb.

"There is Percy," she began. "He is the eldest and the most like me, I suppose. He is quiet and sometimes burdened with a sense of duty, but he loves to paint and sketch, and I have encouraged his talents. His father would not have approved."

"Why not?"

"According to St—my husband, his heir would have no need to embrace his talents. Indeed, he quite ruthlessly suppressed any interests in our sons which did not align with his notion of what proper young lords should know and do. He wanted them to ride, hunt, and know their Latin. That was all."

"I spent my youth learning the family trade of robbing fancy gents and swindling ladies," Damian said, his tone bitter and wry. "Hell of a difference."

The reminder of the vast disparities in their classes settled in her heart like a barb. "Did your mother not keep you from the streets?"

"My mother tossed me into them." He kissed her inner wrist. "From the time I was old enough to walk, she used me as part of her game. She'd distract her victim, and I'd filch a purse or anything I could. It was the only talent that made me worth filling my belly and keeping me under her roof."

"Oh, Damian." How she ached for him, to have been so ill-treated by his own mother, the woman who should have been protecting him. "I am sorry."

"Don't be, love." He kissed the top of her hand. "I learned a great many lessons from my mother, and when I was old enough to leave, I took those lessons and the coin I'd been hiding from her, and I ran. Now tell me about the rest of your family. I fancy the notion of a mother who cares for her children. It makes me happy to hear the love in your voice when you speak of them."

And it saddened her to think he had never heard that same love in the voice of his own mother. That he had been treated as a burden and made to steal on behalf of her. He was a prideful man, however, and she knew he would not appreciate her pity.

"There is also Joanna," she said, continuing with her children by age. "She loves to read, and she is quite intrepid. She has my penchant for adventure, which is often a source of consternation for me. One of her recent scrapes involved falling out of a tree she had been climbing in the gardens.

Gideon is the youngest and the most inquisitive. He is inordinately fond of birds. He also acquired a rather unusual bit of speech from your young Master Davy."

That was putting it politely.

Damian grimaced. "My apologies. However, you did insist on taking the lad into your home."

Indeed, she had.

"And so suffer my reward." She smiled. "Actually, I like the scamp."

"As do I," he admitted. "I see myself in him, when I was a lad that age."

"You have a good heart, Damian Winter," she said softly.

His countenance grew serious and intent. "If you keep looking at me that way, I'm going to have to roll you to your back and make love to you again."

She refused to look away. If this was to be their last night, she was going to be greedy. She did not want to waste a second of it.

"Do you promise?"

He grinned and rolled them as one until she was on her back and he was settled atop her, between her thighs. "I most certainly do."

* * *

They are a part of you, Mira.

Damian's words haunted her the entirety of her journey back to Tarlington House. He had asked after her children. By the time she reached the imposing façade, her cheeks were wet with tears.

Tears for what she longed for so desperately.

Tears for what she could never have.

The Duchess of Stanhope had never been meant to experience love. Hers was an existence mired in duty and propriety. She lived above reproach. Damian Winter must never discover who she truly was.

He was too perceptive, and far too much a danger.

She could never see him again.

Tomorrow, she promised herself grimly. She would send him a note as soon as she could bring herself to write one, explaining as best as she could. It was wrong, and she would hate every moment of writing the words which would ultimately tell him goodbye, of abridging their passion into a tidy, finished volume.

But it was what she had to do.

If there was anything Mirabel knew, it was duty. She had always done that. Nothing would change now. Her children had to come first.

CHAPTER 10

*D*emon was restless.
　　On edge.
Angry.

Nay. To the devil with angry. He was bloody well outraged. Furious. Irritated. Nettled. Annoyed.

Frustrated. That was what he was.

He was seated in Gen's office, trying not to think about the fact that days had passed since he had last seen—and bedded—Mira. Three, to be precise. Also trying not to think about the note she had sent him the day after he had last seen her, one which he had been reluctant to believe meant what he had suspected it did.

That she had put an abrupt end to their arrangement.

A fortnight of clandestine meetings, of bedding her everywhere and anywhere he could at Lady Fortune, of losing his heart to her, had been reduced to a dismissive note. He still did not know her true identity beyond her first name, and she had already decided they were at an end.

He pulled the scrap of paper from the desk, the words already seared upon his memory.

Thank you for all you have done. I shall always remember our time together fondly.
Respectfully yours,
Mirabel

She had not signed the letter as Mira, but used her full name instead. After spending each evening together—nights of lovemaking unlike any he had ever experienced in his life—she had sent him two cursed sentences.

He ground his molars. The urge to crumple the paper was strong. To toss it into the grate and watch it catch flame. But it had come from *her*, and because he was a stupid, hopeless sod, he was loath to destroy it. It also held the faintest hint of her exotic floral scent. Not that he had held it to his nose, desperate for a hint of her.

Who was he fooling? Of course he had done so, and more than once.

That was how much the woman had crept past his defenses, infecting his blood as surely as any poison. The question now was what was he to do about it? Find another lover? Forget about the woman who had destroyed him with her passion this last, charmed fortnight?

Christ. There was no easy answer to his dilemma. Nor was there a good one. He could not deny; this ending nettled.

A knock sounded on the office door, startling him from his ruminations. He stuffed the note into a pocket in the breast of his coat.

"Come," he called, thinking it must not be Davy on the other side, for the lad tended to simply appear without warning.

The better he could hear Demon talking to himself, he supposed.

The portal opened to reveal his half brother Gavin, who sauntered in with the self-assured gait of a man who knew he had the world by the ballocks. And so he did. Gav was a champion prizefighter the likes of which London had never seen. He had never lost a match. The wenches loved him, and so did the lords who wagered on his bouts. A Gavin Winter match was guaranteed to be a square thing.

"Gav." Pleased to see him and equally desperate for a distraction, Demon rose and rounded the desk to embrace his brother and give him a firm slap on the back.

Gavin, who was taller and broader and generally possessed the build of a barbarian, thumped him back with so much force, he knocked a cough out of Demon.

"Oh, Christ. Too hard, was it?" Gavin stepped back. "Sorry, old cuff. Didn't mean to make you nap the bib."

Demon was older than Gavin by a year, and yet, their almost inconsequential age difference was a common source of nettling between them.

"I wasn't crying, you arse," Demon said, giving Gav a brotherly jab in the ribs with his elbow.

"Looked upset when I came in," Gav countered.

Gavin Winter could smash a man with his fist, no question. But he was also damned good at reading a man's mood.

"Head's aching," he lied. "Took a knock to the old knowledge box a few days past."

"Aye. Wine merchant, Hugo. The crooked bastard who was cheating you?"

"Gen told you?" he asked needlessly. It was a foregone conclusion that Gen would have spoken to her brother about it.

She and Gav were the only two bastard Winter siblings who shared a mother. Not that anyone would have told they were full-blooded siblings by having a look at the pair of them. Where Gen was fair-haired, Gavin's hair was dark as the night. Her eyes were light blue and Gav's were bright green.

"Gen and Dom both," Gav confirmed. "Devil and Blade too, at various times. No secrets to be had in this family."

Demon ought to have known that. Although they had found each other at different times, their bond was deep and true. The inkings they shared attested to that. The only one of them who didn't have any was Gen, and that was on account of her being the one with the needle and also being the one who couldn't bear the sight of her own blood.

"Like a bunch of old hens, the lot of you," Demon grumbled. "Clucking and pecking."

Gavin flattened a hand to his heart in mock outrage. "If I was to be any sort of fowl, I'd be a rooster on account of my big—"

"Enough," he interrupted.

"—beak," Gavin finished with a grin. "Here now. What did you think I was going to say?"

He glared at his brother. "Was there a reason for your visit? You didn't say."

"Gen told me you've gone and lost your heart to one of the ladies."

Mother of all saints, this was all he needed. He could only assume Gen had good intentions in involving Gav. However, the visit had poor timing.

"Gen is wrong," he said, clenching his jaw.

"Gen is never wrong," Gav countered.

Not incorrectly, either. Their sister was a wise woman. Every Winter brother held her in highest esteem.

He sighed. "Doesn't matter, either way. The lady has made her lack of interest known."

Gav raised a brow. "Demon Winter, the man who can seduce any woman in London out of her petticoats, has been rejected?"

It was true that Demon had bedded more than his share of women in his younger days.

His ears went hot. "In the past, I may have enjoyed playing at rantum scantum."

"Christ, you sound like an old woman."

He delivered a playful punch to Gav's arm. "I ain't an old woman."

"How is your sconce after that knock you took?" Gavin asked.

Demon knocked on his head. "Sound as ever."

Except for the part of it that could not seem to keep from thinking endlessly of *her*.

"Sound as a leaking boat out to sea?" his brother teased.

"Seems a reasonable comparison." He paused, taking note that Gavin was remarkably uninjured. No cracked knuckles, no bruised, swollen, or cut face. He was forever engaging in bouts as the moment struck him; to see him utterly unwounded was a rarity. "You haven't any bruises or cuts on that ugly dial plate of yours."

"I'm saving myself for my next fight," Gav explained. "Biggest one of my life. It's to be me against Jeremiah Jones."

"Damn." Demon could not stay the disquiet rising within him. "Jeremiah Jones is dangerous, Gav. His last match was against James McDouglas, and he bloody well killed the man."

It may have taken a day for the blows McDouglas had received in the fight to kill him, but the death had been on Jones' hands just the same. It had been the talk of the East End, and many had been outraged when Jones had not been held accountable.

To think his brother would face Jones…it made fear coil into a cold, sick knot in his gut.

"I've two months to prepare myself," Gav said with a shrug, as if he had no concerns at all. No fear.

Knowing Gav, he probably did have no fear. The man had been born bold and unafraid.

"I don't think you should do it, Gav," he said anyway.

"What did I say?" Gav just grinned. "You sound like an old woman. Good thing for you I've come to save you."

"And what are you saving me from, dear brother?"

"Yourself." Gavin sniffed. "If you have to lose your heart and get leg-shackled, it's got to be to a woman who deserves you. One who doesn't send you a note telling you to sod off."

Demon stiffened. "Who the hell told you that?"

"Davy also paid me a visit," Gavin admitted, sounding reluctant. "The lad is worried for you. Said you were the happiest he's ever seen you, until your ladybird sent you a note, and that was that. Said you've been a right thundercloud ever since."

The little shite was now meddling in his affairs. Demon could not say he was surprised.

"I'm going to make him clean the chamber pots for the rest of his damned life," he growled, not meaning a word of the threat but liking the way it felt to say it.

"He loves you as if you're his father, the scamp does."

Demon's eyes burned. "I reckon I rather love him in the same way."

Gav cuffed him on the ear, and Christ but the blow stung. Demon rubbed his ear, pinning his brother with a glare.

But Gav just shook his head. "You see? An old woman, you are. Come with me, and I'll have you back in proper order."

"Where are we going?" he asked, not that it mattered.

"To get spoony drunk."

Demon rubbed his hand over his chest, above the place where Mira's note now rested. "Plummy plan, brother. Lead on."

* * *

"Will you not at least take some tea?" Octavia asked.

Mirabel's stomach lurched at the notion. "No, thank you."

Ever since she had written to Damian ending their affair, she had been wallowing in misery. A fortnight had passed, and still the ache in her heart had not lessened. But now, a new form of discomfort had emerged. Her stomach was rebelling against her, refusing to keep any sustenance down.

And she was terribly afraid she knew what her more recent ailment presaged.

"A biscuit?" her sister pressed. "You look positively bilious, my dear."

"That is because I am." A violent churn of nausea assailed her. "No biscuits."

She did not think she could eat another morsel of sustenance ever again. Her distress was acute.

"I do hope it is nothing catching." Octavia frowned down at her and pressed the back of her hand to Mirabel's brow. "You do not seem feverish, at least. But I must warn you, if the children are struck low with this same complaint, I shall not be on chamber pot duty for all."

Mirabel had made it no farther than the sitting area of her chamber this morning. She was currently draped in wretched fashion over her chaise longue, afraid to move lest she begin erupting like a volcano once more.

"I do not think you need to concern yourself over the children," she said grimly. "This is the sort of malady which is caused by recklessness of a different nature altogether."

Octavia's dark eyebrows arched. "Surely you are not suggesting what I think you are suggesting."

A whiff of tea reached Mirabel then, making her stomach curdle in stern opposition. "Will you be a darling and move the tray away from me? I cannot bear the scent of it just now."

And that was another sign.

Stomach in upheaval, tired, acute sense of smell...

"Of course." Octavia hastened to heft the tray which a servant had brought a few minutes earlier, moving it to a low table at the far end of the room before hurrying back to Mirabel's side. "But let us return now to your words of a moment ago, dearest sister."

"There may have been an unintended, lasting effect of the evenings I spent at Lady Fortune," she admitted, the notion becoming more real to her now that she was giving voice to her fear she was carrying Damian's child.

"You are saying you are *enceinte*?" Octavia asked, her voice a whisper.

It would have been comical if Mirabel were not feeling so pitiful. And if the ramifications of bearing a child when she had already been widowed for over a year were not so socially ruinous. If she had been worried that her affair with Damian would affect her children before, now...

Mirabel closed her yes. "I believe it possible, yes."

More than possible, but she could not admit that aloud. *Heavens*, she could scarcely admit it to herself.

"Mirabel!" Octavia sounded scandalized. "Are there not means by which one avoids such an effect? I understood a gentleman can place a sheath over his rod to capture the seed. A condom, I believe it is called. Surely your Mr. Winter would have worn one?"

Mirabel groaned. "Pray do not tell me the source of this information. I do not think it can be in those scandalous broadsides of yours."

Octavia's grin was unrepentant. "A lady never reveals her sources. But never mind me. We are speaking of you. Did you not take care?"

"Nothing is certain," she said weakly, not bothering to go into detail.

Some matters were best left private.

But that was the crux of the matter—if she was carrying a child, such matters would not remain private for long.

"What shall you do?" Octavia asked.

Mirabel's stomach lurched. "I do not know just yet."

* * *

Demon hadn't the stomach for the chocolate Davy placed before him on the desk. The moment the rich aroma hit his nostrils, his bread basket mutinied.

He clutched his roiling gut and glared at the lad. "Get it out of here."

"I fetched it for yournabs," Davy said, looking crestfallen. "I know it's your favorite."

It had been his favorite. However, in recent mornings, he preferred spirits to take the edge off the previous evening's over-indulgences.

"Get me some drops of jackey instead," he growled. "Chocolate makes me want to flash the hash."

"Too early for gin, don't you think, yournabs?" the lad asked. "If you're going to cast up your accounts, I'll fetch the pot for you."

Demon dug his fingertips into his throbbing temples with merciless determination. "What did I tell you about calling me yournabs?"

He was being surly as a bear to Davy, and he knew it. But he had spent the time since Mira had sent him that damned letter growing increasingly desolate. He devoted each evening to searching the floor for copper curls and a voluptuous form he'd recognize as far away as from another bloody continent, and every day, he had been disappointed.

Nary a word from her, nor a hint of her, since that godawful morning.

"Apologies, sir," the lad grumbled. "Only trying to show you respect."

He continued glaring, which made his head ache worse. "If you respect me, then you will get me the blue ruin."

He and Gav had also spent every night carousing after Lady Fortune closed for the evening. Drinking himself to oblivion distracted him from thoughts of Mira. Falling into an empty bed without her was not nearly as painful when he promptly passed out. The mornings, however.

Christ, the mornings.

They were getting increasingly rougher. And he was beginning to understand that no amount of time or distraction would change the way he felt about Mira.

He loved her. He loved her, and he did not know her full name.

"I ain't going to fetch blue ruin for you," Davy said, crossing his arms over his puny chest. "Won't do you a bit of good."

"It will do me a world of bloody good," he countered through gritted teeth. "Fetch it, and take this cursed chocolate with you."

"Chocolate is your favorite," Davy countered. "My father was a toss pot. Swilled 'imself to death, 'e did. Don't want to see you doing the same. I likes you more than what I liked 'im."

It was the first time the lad had ever spoken of his sire. Demon had known he was an orphan, of course, but Davy had been quiet about his past thus far. The knowledge melted some of his inner ice, for he cared about the lad, too. *Hell*, he had begun to consider him a son.

"Forgive me, lad," he said, gentling his tone. "I ain't a toss pot. I'm merely…heartbroken."

And if ever there had been a confession he would not have considered himself capable of making, it was that one.

But his stomach and his head were aching, he was bloody desolate, and he no longer had a shred of pride remaining, it would seem.

"You love My Grace, don't you?"

His addled mind did not comprehend. "Grace? I do not know anyone by that name other than my half sister, lad."

"Course you do." The lad rolled his eyes. "Carroty-pated fancy lady? I nabbed 'er ring? Took me to 'er big, fancy 'ouse? You've only been moping over 'er since you laid your peepers on 'er..."

"Mira," he interrupted, hating the way her name sounded, how right it felt on his tongue, even after her defection. "Her name is not Grace, lad. It is Mira."

"Aye, but 'er fancy title." Davy shook his head. "My Grace, it was."

Mother of all saints.

Realization dawned. There was only one title which had Grace in it, and the lad had cocked it up.

Mira was a bloody *duchess*.

Another realization dawned. "Lad, do you think you can find your way back to her fancy house again?"

Davy grinned, revealing his missing tooth. "Davy can find 'is way anywhere, sir."

"Excellent. We've a mission later this afternoon." A plan began to materialize in his mind. "Leave the chocolate with me."

No sense in drowning himself today.

CHAPTER 11

Nothing could have prepared Mirabel for the sight of Damian "Demon" Winter standing in the gold salon at Tarlington House. She hovered on the threshold, blinking, certain her eyes were deceiving her.

But no. They were not. He was here. Longing hit her, fierce and intense.

She would recognize that devastatingly handsome figure anywhere. His hands were clasped behind his back, and he stood at a window, observing the street below. He was clad in a gentleman's polished Hessians, buff pantaloons that showed his muscular calves and thighs to perfection, and a black coat with a light waistcoat beneath, a white cravat tied simply at his throat.

To look at him, one would suppose him a lord.

Her weak stomach knotted. Thank heavens it was the afternoon and she had managed to hold down some tea and toast, but his sudden appearance had her ill at ease. Nor could she tamp down the happiness blossoming within her at the sight of him.

How had it been so long since she had seen him, reveled

in the caress of those knowing fingers, had felt his skillful lips traveling over her body? It seemed an eternity.

"Mr. Winter," she greeted him formally, moving forward with purposeful strides.

Careful, however, to maintain a proper distance between them. There was a different air about him, almost tangible, and her mind and heart were both everywhere, uncertainty about her future, about a future with him, about what she needed to do for her children, making her hands tremble. She laced her fingers together to keep her weakness from showing.

He spun about, unsmiling and serious and quite unlike himself. Nevertheless, he offered her a superb bow. Everything about the man was as refined as his fashion and his gleaming boots.

"Good afternoon," he greeted solemnly, his familiar charm notably absent.

"What are you doing here, sir?" she asked quietly when she reached him.

She stopped near enough to taunt herself with his scent. Not in close enough proximity to surrender to her weakness and touch him. That was imperative. If she were to touch him, she would be lost and she knew it.

"I am paying you a call," he said simply. "Such a thing is customary in your circles, is it not?"

"Of course calls are customary," she managed to say, struggling to keep her expression and her voice bland. Emotionless. To quell all the furious yearning erupting within her. "How did you find me here? Lady Fortune promises anonymity to its patrons. Indeed, such a thing is paramount to both the continued patronage of ladies such as myself and Lady Fortune's future success."

His sensual lips thinned, his countenance becoming an

impassive mask of displeasure. "This has nothing to do with Lady Fortune."

"Then how did you find me?"

"Davy." He quirked a dark brow. "You do recall stealing him away and bringing him to your home before returning him when it became apparent to you just how much trouble the lad is, do you not?"

"My intentions were noble," she defended. "Davy had no wish to remain here, and he made himself clear on the matter by thieving everything within reach until he was caught."

"Aye." He gave an indolent shrug. "Call it as you will, Duchess. If you wanted to keep all your secrets, you should never have brought Davy here."

She had not supposed the scamp would betray her. But then, his loyalty to Damian was clear. It was her own judgment which had been compromised.

"I am beginning to realize the error of my ways," she said.

"In more senses than one, I hope."

His low words, issued in that delicious baritone that still caused shivers to trail down her spine whenever she heard it, made her heart pound and her body ache with remembrance. The passion they had shared had been overwhelming. She had never known such pleasure existed.

She had to tell him about her suspicions. Had to reveal she may be carrying his child. But as she looked at him now, the words refused to find her tongue. When she had informed Stanhope of the success of his visits, she had always done so primly, through letters. Nothing about her previous relationship had been anything like what she had shared with Damian.

What she had ended.

He came nearer before she could speak, deliciously close.

"Why did you disappear, Mira? Why did you leave me with nothing but a note?"

Her heart gave a pang at the rawness in his voice, the vulnerability in his handsome face. "Because I did not dare allow you to persuade me to change my mind."

"You feared I would?"

She wet her lips, wishing he were not standing so near, battering the crumbling rampart of her defenses. "Yes."

But he did not stray from his place before her, nor did he hide the yearning in his eyes, in his voice. "Tell me you do not feel it any longer, Mira. Tell me you do not want me, and I will go."

"I have a duty to my children," she told him as much as she reminded herself.

With that thought came another that almost made her knees buckle. There was likely a child in her womb now, at this moment.

Tell him, urged a voice within.

Tell him now. Do not wait.

"I do not seek to hinder that duty," he told her. "God, Mira. I've missed you."

Her traitorous heart gave her away. He was ever a temptation she could not resist.

"I have missed you as well," she said, swaying toward him, needing his touch, his embrace.

"Mama!"

She jumped back as if she had just been burned, jolting away from him in time to see Gideon bounding into the room with his usual boisterous enthusiasm. The lad could not be made to adopt the calm gait of a gentleman. Everywhere he went, he galloped like a horse.

"Gideon," she said weakly. "Why are you not with Clark?"

The replacement of Walters had only just begun several days before, and poor Clark, while possessing a kinder demeanor than her predecessor and infinitely more tolerance for her charges, also seemed to be easily thwarted by Mirabel's intrepid youngest child.

"I needed to ask you a question," he said, studying Damian with open curiosity. "My apologies, Mama. I did not know you had a visitor."

Mirabel was struck in that moment, caught between two worlds, between the Mirabel she wanted to be and between the Duchess of Stanhope she had always been. The Duchess of Stanhope would not introduce Mr. Damian Winter to her son. But then, neither would the Duchess of Stanhope have fallen in love with him.

Mirabel had.

And it was that part of her—the truest part—which was keenly aware of Damian's gaze on her, searching. Waiting. He had to know the war she waged.

She hesitated a moment too long.

Damian took a step back, his countenance shuttering, and bowed. "I was just leaving."

His bearing was stiff, his shoulders and jaw tense. Worst of all, she detected the naked hurt on his proud countenance. "You need not go yet, Mr. Winter," she announced suddenly.

Too loudly.

Her voice was unnaturally high, almost shrill. Damian paused, cocking his head at her and scouring her with a searching glance. Her heart beat faster than the wings of a startled bird.

"Mr. Winter, my son, Lord Gideon Manners."

Damian sketched another bow. "Lord Gideon."

Gideon's expression was curious. Mirabel could practically see the wheel of questions spinning in his mind. "Mr. Winter."

The two stared at each other, as if assessing. Damian towered over Gideon, a stark comparison in appearance that was magnified by the darkness of Damian's hair and eyes juxtaposed with Gideon's shock of wheaten hair and the pale, freckled skin he had inherited from Mirabel.

"I was just telling Her Grace about the bird I saw on my way here," Damian said to Gideon in conspiratorial fashion.

He had done nothing of the sort. Mirabel bit her lip.

"What did it look like, sir? I have memorized the names of at least one hundred different birds," Gideon announced with pride.

"It was a fat gray bird with a black marking around his neck," Damian replied with ease.

Mirabel wondered if he had truly seen such a fowl or if he had merely recalled her telling him that her son was fond of birds. Either way, her heart was heavier than it had ever been.

An enthusiastic grin lit up Gideon's face. "That must have been the ring dove, sir. It stays with us the whole year long."

"I do believe the black marking on the little fellow's neck resembled a ring." Damian stroked his jaw, as if in deep contemplation. "You must be correct, my lord."

"I have been studying birds all my life," Gideon said with the sweet hyperbole of a child. It was apparent he wished to impress their visitor.

Gideon had hungered for interaction from Stanhope, from the time he had first been walking about on the unsteady legs of a newborn foal. Stanhope, however, had shown less interest in him than he had in Percy. Gideon was the necessary spare. How Mirabel's heart ached to think of all her sons and daughter had missed.

"Indeed," Damian was saying to her son, as if he, too, found birds an enrapturing subject of discussion. "Do tell me your favorites, Lord Gideon."

Mirabel almost winced. Her son would happily chatter

about birds for days. The only other subject which interested him was the asking of questions.

"There is the red-backed butcherbird," Gideon began. "He snares his dinner on thorns. There is the common crow, which travels in pairs. The sandpiper, who prefers to be near water. The ring ouzel, the bunting—"

"Lord Gideon," interrupted a flustered-sounding Clark, who appeared on the threshold of the salon, her cheeks flushed. "I was searching for you."

It was a timely intervention save the manner in which Clark's gaze traveled over Damian. With something more than curiosity, Mirabel swore. Appreciation? He was a ridiculously handsome man.

"Go with Clark now," she urged her son. "I shall be along presently to see your progress with French."

"I shall tell you more about birds later, Mr. Winter," Gideon said, his tone hopeful.

Mirabel was about to interject when Damian spoke first.

"I should like nothing better, Lord Gideon," he said.

When Gideon and Clark were gone, leaving Mirabel and Damian alone once more, she did not know whether to throw herself into his arms or berate him. Part of her told her to proceed with caution. This was dangerous, new, unexpected territory. The other part of her wanted to throw her arms around him and never let go this time.

"You are looking at me strangely, Mira." His low, beloved voice cut through her inner tumult. "Have I overstepped? Was I not meant to speak with your son? Forgive me. I know I ain't your social equal."

His polish had slipped.

And she loved him for it all the more.

She loved the way he had held her in his arms, the way he had made love to her as if he savored every moment, as if he delighted in her in an elemental sense. She loved the way he kissed her. Loved the way he felt deep inside her. She loved the penchant he had for always making her smile, for finding the strangest, most delicious places on her body she had never known would adore being kissed. She loved his mahogany hair and stirring eyes and sinful lips. She loved his hands, his accent, his occasional dips into cant. She loved that he was himself, without apology.

Except in this instance. Only for her.

"You need not ask my forgiveness, Damian," she said softly. "If anyone should require forgiveness, it is me."

He moved toward her once more. "For tiring of me?"

Is that what he thought of her?

She shook her head, guilt twisting deep within that he could suppose her so fickle. But then, what choice had she given him?

"I never tired of you." The admission spilled from her, making her a bit dizzy.

She should have tried to eat more than toast, but she had not been certain her unsettled stomach would allow it. Her lack of sustenance was wreaking havoc upon her now. But this was familiar territory. Each time she had been with child had been much the same, with the exception of the manner in which her belly had grown. She had been largest when she carried Joanna.

"Then why did you end us?" he asked, his warm, brown stare penetrating. "Could you not have met with me? Could you not have looked me in the eye and told me you wished never to see me again? You say you feared I would persuade you otherwise. If you are so easily persuaded, I reckon you did not want what you asked for."

He was not wrong.

She searched for an explanation that would placate him, before it occurred to her that she was reverting to the Duchess of Stanhope once more. When she and her husband had been at odds, she always deferred to him. Surrendered. It had been easier, more peaceful, than testing him. If she bent and yielded, he would go away. That was not the way of it between herself and Damian. At least, it had not been, and she did not want to make it so.

There was only one answer she could give him: the truth.

"You are right," she confessed, waving her hands about in her agitation. "I did not want to end our arrangement, but I felt that I must do so in the interest of my children. I have built a reputation, you see. All these years, I have been unimpeachable. I have followed all the rules, done everything I should. There has been nary a hint of scandal shadowing my name."

She paused, gathering her courage before continuing. "I am the Duchess of Stanhope, always above reproach. I was being selfish, pursuing you, seeking something I had no right to claim. It was sinful and wrong of me. I am their mother before I am anything else, and I must put their needs, their futures, ahead of everything. Even if…"

Her words trailed off, and she found herself unable to finish them.

"Even if it meant cutting your ties with me," he finished for her. "Even if it meant destroying everything there was between us."

Oh, how she hated his use of the past tense, as if everything they had shared was gone. But then, why would she expect anything different? She had left him. Had put an end to their affair. It was the past.

However, he was still here. And that had to mean something, did it not?

"Mira?" he prodded.

"Yes," she allowed quietly. "Even if it meant destroying what was between us. I…I thought it was for the best."

"Do you still think it is best?" he asked, moving nearer still.

Bringing with him the intoxicating scent that was purely his. "Do you want the truth? I have no notion of what to think any longer."

He took her hands in his, the touch so needed. "Do you still want me?"

"Must you ask?"

"Aye." His expression was grave. "I must. I'll not return here, and I'll never contact you again if I know you are certain and you feel your life is better without me in it."

"I still want you," she said softly.

A life without him in it? She had spent the last fortnight in abject despair. The notion of the rest of her life? It was unthinkable, unbearable.

"Good." He raised her hands to his lips, kissing the knuckles. "I never stopped wanting you, Mira. Hell, I do not think it possible for me to *stop* wanting you. You have found your way into my blood, it seems. The only means by which I have managed to drive you from my mind has been drinking myself to oblivion, and even when I am sotted, you are there, at the edges of my every thought, haunting me."

He had been suffering then, just as much as she had. The knowledge was bittersweet, for it did nothing to assuage their pain or to mend the rift she had created. Nor did it miraculously light a path for her to follow through the darkness.

"I never stopped wanting you either." She gave him a tremulous smile, her foolish heart swelling with love for this man. "It is difficult for me. I have spent my life being a mother and putting all their needs and concerns first. What has happened between the two of us...I never expected to feel so strongly."

"Nor did I." He tugged her into his chest, and she went

willingly, hungering for his sturdy protection, his warmth. He embraced her tightly. "Mira mine, I have never felt for another what I feel for you. It terrifies me to admit this, but I… Hell. I love you. You have my heart. You'll always have my heart, even should you tell me to go to the devil in the next minute."

He loved her? Her arms, which had naturally slid around his lean waist when he pulled her into his body, tightened. Her face was buried in his chest, and she inhaled deeply, savoring his scent, savoring *him*.

"I love you too," she murmured into his cravat.

She had never imagined she would admit that to the charming, wholly unsuitable, elegant, handsome rogue to whom she had lost her heart.

He stilled. "Pardon, Duchess?"

She laughed, but it was half a sob as she tipped her head back to meet his gaze. "Do not call me that, I beg of you."

His expression was solemn. "As you wish, love. Pardon, Mira mine?"

She liked that better. Indeed, she liked that much, much better. Because she wanted to be his. In every way. Always.

Mirabel swallowed hard before repeating the three words. "I love you."

"Thank Christ," he said, then pressed a kiss to her forehead, her nose, her lips. "Say it again."

"I love you," she repeated into his mouth.

His only response was to crush her lips beneath his.

* * *

SHE LOVED HIM.

Fucking, floating hell.

Mira *loved* him.

He did not know what the devil that meant for them.

They were still unequal, and she was conflicted about her duty to her children, which he respected. All he *did* know was the soaring emotions inside his chest. Happiness. Love. Hope, too.

He kissed her with all the feelings he had done his utmost to drown during the time they had been apart. She tasted of tea, floral and sweet and *Mira*. Now, all he wanted to drown in was her. But as all the pent-up need for her clamored through him, he reminded himself he was a guest in her massive, fancy home. That she was a duchess. And that whilst she loved him, she had also been willing to leave him.

He ended the kiss with great reluctance, staring down at her upturned face. Had she grown more beautiful in her absence from his life? *Christ*, it certainly seemed so. He wanted to kiss every freckle on her nose. Wanted to take her in his arms and carry her away with him and never let her go. She was all he wanted.

"I am willing to do whatever you ask of me," he said, swallowing the tattered remnants of his pride. "Tell me what you need."

Her lips were swollen, her eyes wide. "I need to tell you something, Damian."

"Go on," he urged.

Whatever it was, he would weather the news. Nothing could be worse than what he had already endured, a fortnight without her.

"I believe I may be in a delicate condition," she said, her countenance stricken.

Mother of all saints.

"You are carrying my child? Our child?"

"Yes." She nodded, still studying him with care. "Our child."

Wonder burst open inside him, like a spring bud under the warmth of the sun. Ever since the moment he had first laid eyes on her fiery curls and those brilliant blue eyes blazing behind her mask, he had been in the palm of her hand. And now? His joy was radiant, uncontrollable.

Until something occurred to him.

"Were you going to tell me?" he asked, needing to know. "If I had not called upon you today, Mira, would you have told me?"

"The discovery is a recent one. I would not have kept our child a secret from you, but I was also trying to decide how best to proceed, given my place in society and your position in the East End."

Hurt sliced through him. "I ain't good enough for a duchess."

"You are good enough." She sighed, her lower lip trembling, her eyes glistening with unshed tears. "You are my better in every way. You have been nothing but sweet and considerate and wonderful to me, and I have rewarded you by running away because I was not strong enough."

"To the devil with that." He caught her chin in his thumb and forefinger, tenderly stroking her soft skin. "You are stronger than you think, Mira. You were bold enough to break society's rules when you came to me looking for a lover."

"But Lady Fortune is circumspect," she argued. "I was wearing a mask. To you, I was nothing more than a number and half a face."

"You were the woman I have been searching for," he countered, caressing her cheek now, grateful for his lack of gloves, for the warmth of her searing him, unobstructed. "You astounded me, put me under your spell. I had to have you."

"You have me now."

"In my arms, aye." He pulled her nearer, lowering his forehead to hers. "But what of more, Mira? I was born a bastard. I'll not do the same to a child of mine. Will you marry me?"

"Yes."

Her affirmation filled him with a swelling sense of relief.

"Thank Christ." He kissed her nose. Kissed every bloody adorable freckle he could find.

"But there is much we need to concern ourselves with," she said, and his happiness was like an ascension balloon suddenly plummeting back to the earth. "I am older than you."

"You are also more beautiful."

"Ten years can be something of a difference."

"I don't give a goddamn about the years, Mira."

She sighed. "I have three children."

He kissed the tip of her nose. "You are about to have five."

Her brow furrowed. "Forgive me for finding fault in your arithmetic, but it shall only be four."

"You are forgetting Davy." He kissed the constellation of freckles over her cheekbone. "The imp needs a proper father and mother."

"He does." She rubbed her cheek along his in the fashion of a cat. "I could never forget Davy. Do you suppose he will thieve the candlesticks this time?"

"He'll not be thieving at all if I have my way." He frowned, raising his head once more to study her. "It won't matter anyway, because he won't be living here in your palace."

"It is hardly a palace, Damian. But if not here, where shall he live?"

Excellent bloody question. "Where we all will be living."

"Why not here?" she asked.

He had not come to her intending to offer marriage. *Hell*, he did not know what he had come here for, other than to see her. To touch her, hold her. To persuade her to return to his life. But how swiftly everything had changed.

The moment she had revealed she was carrying a child, he had known that any promises he had made to himself to allow Mira to set the pace would have to be broken. He would not allow his child to be born as he had been, on the wrong side of the blanket. Still, there remained the matter of how they would actually make a union between an East End ruffian and a duchess work.

"I don't belong in a place like this, Mira," he told her as gently as possible. "I will break something."

"Then we will buy a replacement."

"I will say the wrong words."

"I say the wrong words regularly." She kissed his jaw.

"I'll never be a lord."

"That's bloody good, because I do not want one. I want *you*."

"Curse you, woman," he growled without heat. "You ought to watch your vulgar tongue."

The grin curving her lips was seduction personified. "I can think of other uses for my tongue."

He groaned, his cock going instantly hard. "It has been too long since I've made love to you, Mira mine. Do not taunt me here in the midst of your salon."

"Do you agree?" She kissed his ear, then the swath of neck above his cravat.

"When you are the one asking, I will agree to anything," he admitted before he sealed his mouth over hers.

CHAPTER 12

A meeting of the Winter siblings had been called to order.

It was not often that all the Winters assembled in the same room at the same time. Indeed, it was quite rare, given that they were mostly wed and their lives were consumed with the whirlwind of duties, children, and for some of them, country estates. But Demon had requested the presence of his siblings today with a most important purpose in mind.

He stared at the assemblage seated before him in their older brother Dev's townhome, which had been chosen on account of the size of his drawing room. Fitting twelve Winters into a room proved no easy feat. Except, today, there were only eleven. Ten expectant faces were turned toward him.

"Where is Gavin?" he asked, looking at Gen, for Gav often kept her more apprised of his plans than anyone else.

Gen looked about. "He hasn't come? I have not heard from him for several days now, I believe. Not since I last saw him at Lady Fortune, dragging you off to drown yourselves in blue ruin."

She was dressed in a gown today rather than her customary breeches, cravat, and boots, which was surprising in itself. Not nearly as surprising as her words, however.

"That was a week ago," he observed. "Has no one seen Gav since?"

A chorus of responses rose from the remainder of the Winters. The resounding consensus was *no*. They had not. None of them.

The heavy weight of dread settled in Demon's gut. "None of you?"

The Winters collectively shook their heads, a sea of solemn countenances.

"Hell," he muttered to himself. Then louder, for the room to hear, "I sent a note round to him, but I never received a response. That was nothing out of the ordinary, however. Gav often ignores me and later appears."

"I am certain he will arrive at any moment now," said his half sister Christabella, a duchess in her own right and the more hopeful and sweet-natured of all Demon's siblings.

"Of course he will," drawled their half sister Grace, Lady Aylesford with a roll of her eyes.

"He has a bout in the next three weeks," Gen said. "He is bound to turn up."

"Jeremiah Jones," growled their half brother Dom, his lip curled in disgust. "A bad halfpenny, that match. I've warned him, but the stubborn arse refuses to listen."

"Aye. I warned him as well," offered their half brother Devil, a tall, hulking beast who ordinarily towered over them. Today, he was seated on a particularly feminine-looking settee, which rendered him on the same level as all the rest of their siblings.

"As did I," chimed in Blade, another bastard Winter brother, this one fair-haired and silver-tongued. At least, he had been the latter until he had recently fallen in love and gotten himself leg-shackled to a lady.

What was it about Winters marrying into the quality? Polite society likely sneered at them all, thinking they had all married to improve their social standing. However, they had, each one of them, fallen in love along the way, regardless of the manners in which their marriages had unfolded.

All of them except Demon and Gavin, that was.

But Demon was about to rectify that, and he was going to wed a goddamn duchess.

Gav, however…

Gav remained a mystery, just like his whereabouts.

"He is one quarter hour late," Dev pointed out. "It does not seem as if he will be arriving."

"Perhaps something is amiss," suggested their half sister Pru.

"It would certainly seem so," agreed Bea, the smallest and youngest of the legitimate Winter siblings.

"Regardless of wherever he is, I would have it be known that I think he will decimate any opponent," offered their half sister Eugie, Countess of Hertford.

"Of course he will," Gen agreed. "Jones is a formidable fighter, but Gav is a champion."

Silence reigned.

Demon looked to the door, then back to the waiting faces of his siblings. *Damn it*, something did not feel right about Gav's absence.

"I will go to his rooms after this meeting," he announced, knowing he would not feel at ease unless he did, and also knowing Gen would be the first to volunteer herself, despite the potential danger she may face.

Gav delighted in taking rooms in the seamiest parts of the rookeries. He claimed it kept him at the ready and helped him to hone his skills as a bareknuckle boxer. Instinct, timing, always being aware, training his body and his mind into an expert weapon. That was what Gav did.

"I'll come with you," Gen volunteered, her voice tinged with concern.

"You'll do nothing of the sort," Dom and Devil snapped at their sister simultaneously, sparing Demon the task.

"I ain't going to say a word," Blade offered, grinning. "You cannot tell Gen Winter what to do."

"Yes," Gen agreed. "Though I am no longer Gen Winter."

"Hell." Blade flashed her a shamefaced grin. "Lady Sundenbury."

"I am going to proceed with the reason for this meeting, if it suits my sisters and brothers, Gav notwithstanding since he is not present."

Once more, a chorus of agreement rose from his siblings.

"Deuced hard to believe there are twelve of us," he commented. "Even without Gav, this room is bloody well filled."

"I wonder if there shall be any more," Christabella said, grinning unrepentantly. "Our father seemed to be…prolific."

The rest of them loosed a collective groan.

"I think twelve of us is all London can bear," Demon said, smiling right back at his sister, who truly was a ray of sunshine in the gloom.

Then again, mayhap he had a special fondness for fiery-haired women.

Beginning with one in particular.

Which reminded him of the reason for this bloody meeting in the first place.

"I am going to be married," he announced.

The room went silent.

Except for Gen, who hooted like a damned owl, clapping her hands and grinning. "I hesitate to say I told you so, dearest brother. However, I did tell you, did I not? You fell in love."

His cheeks went hot. "Gen."

"What?" She shrugged, looking like the cat who had ventured into the cream. "You are marrying your Mira, are you not?"

Now his ears were burning. He pinned his sister with a glare. "Yes. I am."

And thank Christ for that. He could still scarcely believe his fortune. It had been days since she had agreed to marry him, and he felt as if he were walking about in a dream.

If it was a dream, he damned well did not want to wake.

A cacophony exploded in the drawing room as ten Winter siblings attempted to speak at once. Demon only caught snippets.

"Who is Mira?"

"When are the nuptials?"

"Another Winter falls."

"Too much temptation at Lady Fortune?"

There was more, but Demon silenced them with a raised hand. "Quiet, if you please. The reason I have asked you all to assemble here is that I am aiming to marry the Duchess of Stanhope in the next month, and doing so will be a deuced delicate matter."

Delicate matter.

He could scarcely believe his own tongue.

There were gasps.

"The Duchess of Stanhope?" Eugie asked. "I scarcely believe it. She is a notorious prude."

He could attest to the fact that Mira was not, in fact, a prude. But he was a gentleman. Of sorts. And he would defend his future wife's honor to the death.

"We are in love," he said simply.

"The Duchess of Stanhope," Christabella repeated.

He nodded. "There is only one, I trust."

No one spoke. Ten faces stared at him, Gen the only one amongst them who was beaming and wiping the tears from her cheeks. That was likely to be attributed to her delicate condition. For if anyone was disinclined to maudlin sentiment, it was she.

"What do you require of us?" Dev asked into the silence. "Ask, and it shall be done."

Gratitude and pride swept over Demon. Whilst the bastard Winters and their legitimate counterparts had not always been close, time and determination had forged their loyalties. He was thankful to be a part of this vast family, and what a strange thought that was for a lad who had once been adrift, with no hope of a family aside from his mother, who did not deserve the title.

"I need your aid," he confessed. "For her sake, and for the sake of our children, I need to learn how to mingle with the quality. I need to know how to be a gentleman. Gen, I am going to have to bow out of running Lady Fortune, but I have already spoken to Tiny Tom, and he assures me he can carry on without me."

Gen dabbed at her nose with a handkerchief. "He is more than capable, Demon."

"That is another matter," he said, reminded by his sister's use of the only name he had known as a man grown. "My Christian name is Damian. I'll be answering to it now, instead of Demon."

Whilst Mira had made not a single demand of him, nor one request, he was making these changes for her sake. She would have a difficult enough path to traverse, the proper duchess marrying a rogue from the rookeries. He had no wish to make anything worse. He wanted to make certain she would bear as little strain and scandal as possible. And in so doing, their children as well.

For that was how he had already come to think of their family. Percy, Joanna, Gideon, Davy, and the babe. His heart was so damned full, so unexpectedly, beautifully overflowing. Not that he was about to announce that to the group gathered before him, regardless of how much he loved their miserable hides as well.

"Fair enough," said Dom. "Damian suits you far better than Demon these days anyhow."

He rather thought so as well. Mira had changed him. Softened him. Had helped him to find happiness and love in a way he had never imagined possible. A lump rose in his throat, and his eyes began to sting, but he would not unman himself by weeping before his siblings.

"If any of you can help us to smooth the waters for Mira's sake, and for the sake of the children, I would be forever indebted to you."

"We will help you in any fashion we can," Dev reassured him.

"We are Winters," added Grace.

"Helping each other is what we do," Devil agreed.

Demon nodded. "Thank you. I love you all."

"We love you too, brother," said ten voices in unison.

The missing eleventh voice was a mystery that troubled him, but for now, he was well pleased with the vows of his siblings. With the Winter family wealth and growing connections behind him, and a little polish of his own, he would be able to at least attempt to become the husband Mira deserved.

If nothing else, he would always be the man who loved her.

But he was determined to fight like hell for all the rest.

Which also reminded him. "Do any of you have a room I might use until Mira and I wed? I have decided it would be best if I am not living above a gaming hell—albeit one as secretive and above reproach as Gen's."

"Stay with us here," Dev invited.

"I will have a guest," he said. "A lad I am aiming to take under my wing."

As long as the lad in question would agree to it, that was. Demon had yet to put the question to him.

* * *

THERE HAD BEEN no sign of Gav at his rooms. Demon had inquired after his brother with the landlord, who had not seen Gavin recently, but who—soused on ale at all times of the day—seemed to possess a foggy memory at best. Demon had left a note for Gav and had returned to Lady Fortune, still plagued by the grim fear that something was afoot with Gav.

However, it was not entirely out of character for Gav to disappear for a few days, particularly if he had found a woman to distract him. Demon decided to put his concerns aside for the moment in favor of having a talk with Davy.

He called the lad into Gen's office, and they began with Demon explaining he was going to be leaving his position at the ladies' gaming hell.

Davy crossed his arms over his chest and cast a mutinous glare in Demon's direction. "Wish I never told you where My Grace lives."

"Her Grace," Demon corrected gently.

"As you say." The lad's lip curled. "You're leaving Lady Fortune for good?"

"For good," Demon echoed.

"No more running the floor?"

"No more running the floor."

Davy's eyes narrowed. "And what of Chef? What of the

boxes for the poor? You aim to just be a fancy man, too good for any of the rest of us what's been down in the dirt with you all this time?"

"I have no hopes of being a fancy man, and I most certainly do not consider myself better than any of you. As for the rest, Chef will continue to cook excellent food, and the boxes will continue to be distributed. Tiny Tom is going to be taking charge, and he is a good man."

"What if 'e makes me empty chamber pots? What then?"

"He is not going to make you do anything, lad," Demon said gently, resting a hand on the scamp's thin shoulder. "Not if you do not wish it."

Davy's eyes narrowed more. "What's that opposed to mean, yournabs?"

"*Sup*posed," he corrected, "and we have already talked about yournabs. I'll never be a lord, Davy."

"You're acting like one," the lad grumbled, eyes cast to the floor.

But Demon spied the sheen in them and recognized it all too well. Tears.

"But I am not one. Instead, I am..." His words trailed off as a fit of emotion seized him, for he had been about to say *I am the man who wants to be a father to you.* "Hell, lad. I care about you. I care about what happens to you. I cannot leave you here when I move on. We are quite similar, you and I, and I see so much of myself in you when I was of an age. Know this, lad, I do not wish to take the place of your father, and neither would Mira take your mother's place. She and I have spoken, and we have decided together that we would be happy for you to join our family."

The lad was silent, simply staring at Demon as if he had sprouted a second head. Until at long last, he broke the silence.

"I filch," Davy said. "I steal whatever I can, and I am right good at it, sir."

The lad was an unparalleled pickpocket, and he knew it. He seemed to possess a rare, incredible talent for distracting someone whilst quietly robbing them of their belongings.

"You are a pickpocket because you like the attention it brings you," Demon said. "Your thievery was borne out of necessity, but that is no longer the case. You now have a roof over your head, plenty of bread in your belly, and a warm place to sleep. I ain't a fool, lad. Nor am I so different from you. I know what you did and why, because I've done it all myself."

Davy's wheaten brows rose. "You have?"

"I have," he confirmed grimly, for he did not prefer to speak of his past. But when the rare occasion merited a retelling, he would allow it, even as it crushed him to recall those painful years. "But all that is immaterial, lad. You need a family and a home, a true home. We can give you that. We *want* to do so. All you have to do is say *aye*."

"I'll not be a servant at 'er fancy 'ouse," Davy said with a scowl.

Demon's heart squeezed. He patted the lad's shoulders. "I said family, scamp. You'll be no servant. You will be our... hell, if you will permit it, you will be our son."

There. He had said the word. *Son.* It seemed to hover in the air, an invitation he was not altogether sure he should have extended. Not because he regretted it, and not because it was not what he wished, but because he did not want to pressure Davy into making a decision he did not want to make.

"You need not think of yourself as such," he hastened to say. "Not if it isn't what you want."

"Son?" Davy tucked his chin and stared at his feet, shuffling them.

"Only if you wish it," Demon reiterated. "We will not force you into making any decisions you may regret. All we want you to know is that we are more than happy for you to make your home with us, for you to join our family as our son."

"I do."

The lad spoke the two words so swiftly and quietly that Demon was certain he had misheard. He leaned forward. "I beg your pardon, scamp?"

Davy smiled. "I want to be your son."

If Demon's heart had been swelled and overflowing before, it was now a cursed waterfall. An endless flow of emotion.

He patted Davy on his thick shock of blond hair. "You already are, lad. I suspect you have been so for quite some time."

Davy did something entirely unexpected then. He threw his arms around Demon and held him tight.

"Thank you," he said, sniffling in uncharacteristic fashion for Davy. "You 'ave paid me a great honor."

Demon shook his head. "You have paid me a greater one, Davy. By far."

* * *

As she had so many times before, Mirabel found herself at a ball.

This time, however, she had been eager to attend. She wanted to be here. And not because she wished to dance or watch the young debutantes and bucks swirling about on the dance floor. But because the man she loved was in attendance.

Damian was here.

The candles in the ballroom at Mr. Deveraux Winter's

townhome were blazing. A glittering crush of London's finest had amassed for the impromptu masque he and his wife, the beautiful Lady Emilia Winter, were holding. The stage was set, and all the revelers in attendance were whispering about the mysterious man dressed in midnight black, his handsome face partially obscured by his silken mask.

The same mysterious man who bowed before her now as the orchestra struck up the strains of a waltz.

"Your Grace," he said, his deep, beloved voice like velvet gliding over her.

She curtseyed. "Mr. Winter."

"I believe this dance is mine?"

"This one and every other," she said.

"For shame, Duchess," he returned with a teasing air. "That sounds positively scandalous. You ought to know you cannot dance with the same gentleman all evening."

"Of course I do." She smiled as he led her to the dance floor, her heart feeling as if it glowed from within, beating with so much love. "You are the only man I *want* to dance with."

Many curious stares were upon them, just as she had known they would be, for it was a well-known truth that the Duchess of Stanhope did not dance. Mirabel had taken great care in her toilette this evening, fastening the Stanhope sapphires at her throat and ears, her flaming hair on display in an elaborate coiffure. Her mask, too, was small, revealing almost her entire face. She wanted there to be no doubt about her identity, because after this evening, all London would know the Duchess of Stanhope had fallen in love with a dashing stranger.

Their whirlwind courtship was to begin this evening, thanks to the Herculean efforts of the Winter family. They had worked together, using their newly cemented society influence to pull together a masque ball in less than a week's time and to ensure that all London would be desperate for an invitation. Mirabel was deeply grateful for the man taking her in his arms now, and for his siblings as well.

There would still be a great deal of whispers surrounding the Duchess of Stanhope's hasty nuptials to Mr. Damian Winter. Indeed, she was certain there would be several scandalmongering broadsides bearing her likeness in the weeks to come. However, planting the seed of their love story this evening would go a long way to blunt the worst of the gossip.

Their hands entwined over their heads, and the warmth and strength of his arm around her was so wonderful. As they began to whirl about the dance floor, she was mesmerized by his dark stare locked on hers, by his fluid, masculine grace. They had been practicing this waltz ever since Devereaux and Lady Emilia had decided upon hosting this ball as a means of providing Mirabel and Damian with a proper introduction.

And the practice was certainly reaping its rewards now.

He had her breathless. Speechless.

"I could not bloody well wait to have you in my arms tonight, love," he said as he led them through a series of steps. "I have missed having you in my bed."

Her cheeks went warm. "Now who is being scandalous, Mr. Winter?"

He grinned. "I never said I wasn't scandalous."

They twirled together in perfect harmony.

"Thank you for going to so much effort to protect me and the children," she said softly, feeling dizzied from the combination of the dance and the elation rising within her.

"I would do anything for you, Mira mine. Even if it means learning how to keep from tripping over my own bloody feet and spinning all over ballrooms. Even if it means living in a palace and trying not to break all the damned china." He paused, wincing. "And even if it means I need to make an extra effort to control my tongue."

"I like your tongue. Never change it."

His grin deepened. "Good to know, love. I shall reacquaint you with it soon."

They whirled about some more.

"Wicked man."

"I am a wicked Winter, you know."

Mirabel threw back her head and laughed as they waltzed, not caring there were eyes upon them. Not caring who would whisper. When the laughter fled her, she was still dancing in the arms of the man who had shown her happiness and love existed.

She gazed up into that warm, brown gaze, her joy unrestrained. "And I would not have you any other way, my darling man."

He winked. "You may have me any way you like, and as often as possible."

She was sure she was flushing to the roots of her hair. But she had never been happier. And all that truly mattered was love.

* * *

THE NEXT MORNING, Octavia rushed to Mirabel's sitting room with the broadside she had managed to acquire.

Triumphantly, she held it up for Mirabel's inspection. "You are the talk of London, sister."

The broadside depicted the crush of the masque ball and showed a red-haired woman wearing a sash bearing the name *The Duchess of Ice*. The Stanhope sapphires were at her throat, exaggerated and large. A handsome, dark-haired man towered over her, dressed all in black, his face obscured by a mask. They were pictured in an embrace, hands linked as they danced the waltz, whilst the crowd around them openly leered and stared.

Mirabel read the title of the caricature aloud. "*The Heart Thief.* For once, Octavia, I approve of your love of gossip."

Octavia grinned unrepentantly. "You are most welcome."

EPILOGUE

As had become a nightly ritual, Demon, Mira, Octavia, Percy, Joanna, Davy, and Gideon were gathered together in the gold salon at Tarlington House to listen to Mira's unending story. The children were on the rug at the hearth, Octavia among them, and Demon and Mira were seated together on a settee. Her ever-burgeoning belly rendered it difficult indeed for her to rise from the floor, and he was happy to settle at her side, his arm drawn around her waist, as the children listened in rapture.

All was happy in Demon's world, and that was how he preferred it. His siblings were contented, he thought. Though what had happened with Gav had been most surprising of all. And Demon? Well, he had discovered a newfound passion to right the wrongs in the world in any way he could. For tonight, however, all he wanted was to savor his family.

This evening, it was Percy's turn to continue the tale. The eldest of their children was reading aloud from the journal in which he had carefully written his contribution.

"A dragon swooped down from the sky," Percy announced.

"Did it have scales?" Gideon asked, interrupting.

"'Course it has scales," Davy said, taking care to pronounce his *h*. "All dragons do."

The lad had been working hard in the schoolroom, and it showed.

"Are dragons part fish?" Gideon queried next.

"No, dear," Mira said, smiling indulgently. "Dragons and fish are decidedly unrelated."

"Why do they both have scales, then?" the lad asked.

"Dragons are not real," his sister interjected. "Do stop interrupting, Gideon. We were just approaching the good part of the story. Something is about to happen."

But her younger brother remained undeterred. "Did you know that herons eat fish?"

"They also eat lads who ask too many questions," Percy said pointedly.

Gideon frowned. "You said that about lions, too, but Mama said it wasn't true."

His siblings groaned. Demon could not contain his chuckle. Life with his family was certainly never boring. Octavia shook her head at her nephew's antics.

"Herons do not eat lads who ask too many questions," Demon said. "Dragons, however...well, I am afraid dragons *do*."

Percy guffawed. The eldest of their children was far more reserved than his younger siblings, but Demon had been making progress with him just as he had with Joanna and Gideon. His sister-in-law Octavia had warmed to him immediately, and he was grateful for her aid in adjusting the children to their new family arrangement.

She was an excellent and doting aunt. Also, something of a hoyden, with a penchant for sneaking about and an unabashed curiosity about the rookeries. But that was something he would only concern himself with if it proved necessary.

Gideon's eyes narrowed. "Papa! You are bamming me."

Demon smiled, warmth seeping through his heart just as it did whenever the lad called him Papa. Joanna and Davy had gradually begun referring to him as Papa as well, and on each occasion, his heart seemed as if it had grown ten times too large for his chest. He did not think he would ever grow tired of hearing that title. Or the other one which had also become his proudest—husband.

"Mayhap I *am* teasing you, lad," he allowed, winking. "For now, I do believe it is time for your brother to continue reading his story."

"Thank you, Papa," Percy said.

Everything within him froze. The young duke stared back at him with a small smile and gave him a nod, as if acknowledging the importance of the moment. Demon's eyes were burning, but he nodded in return, trying to maintain his composure.

Percy went back to reading his story, and Demon felt his wife's gaze. He turned to find her eyes searing him, love shining in their bright-blue depths. Her hand found his, their fingers linking.

I love you, she mouthed to him.

He sniffled, trying to hold back the tears of sheer happiness. *I love you*, he said, just as soundlessly.

And as for his heart?

Well.

It was now at least twenty times too large for his chest, he was sure of it.

* * *

Mirabel concluded writing in her journal for the evening as she waited for Damian to finish poring over his articles and treatises as he spent several hours doing each night. Her husband wanted to stand for Parliament. It was a far cry from the dashing man who had run Lady Fortune. She could not be prouder of the man he was, of the loving father he had become to their brood of children, and of the wonderful husband he was to Mirabel herself.

She had spent the entirety of her first marriage lonely, oppressed, and bitter at the path her life had taken and the unfeeling man she had wed. But Damian was her second chance, and he had been worth the wait.

She stood just as the door to her chamber opened. Her husband crossed the threshold, closing the portal at his back. He was dressed in a midnight banyan, every bit as sinfully handsome as he had been on the first day she had met him in the private room at Lady Fortune. More so, in fact. His mahogany hair was all tousled waves she loved to run her fingers through. His dark eyes brimmed with sensual promise. And his lips were curved in a smile that never failed to make desire simmer to life within her.

"Why so serious, love?" he asked as he reached her. "Has something upset you?"

She shook her head, her hand resting on the swell of her belly, which seemed to grow more prominent each day. "Of course not. I was merely thinking of how happy you make me and how wonderfully dashing you are."

His arms slid around her, drawing her nearer, until her belly prohibited additional proximity. "Tell me more."

She laughed, settling her hands on his broad shoulders. The natural ease between them was an endless source of joy for her. Mirabel had never imagined marriage could be as it was between herself and Damian—so effortless, and yet so powerful. Their bond ran true and deep.

"I was also thinking of how thankful I am that I listened to my sister's ridiculous suggestion and found you at Lady Fortune."

"That was one of her better ideas," he agreed easily, dipping his head to kiss her.

The kiss turned quickly carnal as she opened for his questing tongue and raked her nails down the fabric covering his chest. He groaned, then nipped at her lower lip. She wanted him to devour her, and she wanted to consume him. Desire pooled between her thighs. She was already wet and aching for him, just from one kiss, her nipples hard beneath her dressing gown, her sensitive breasts feeling swollen with need.

As he kissed his way down her jaw to her throat, her fingers made an exploration of their own. Down his lean torso, to where his cock was thick and heavy, jutting high against the billowing cotton of his banyan. She gave him a squeeze, the action tearing a moan from the both of them.

"I have been waiting all bloody day to make love to you again," he said against her skin.

"You made love to me a few hours ago in the music room," she pointed out breathlessly.

He feverishly worked at the buttons on her gown, plucking them open with a speed that bespoke of his desperation. "Four hours, to be precise. Four hours too long ago."

With the children distracted and Octavia off to pay a call upon one of her friends, Mirabel had lured Damian into the music room with the intention of seducing him. Thankfully, her delicate condition no longer upset her stomach. However, it did have a new effect upon her. One her husband had not seemed to mind, since he was every bit as ravenous for her as she was for him. They had wound up tangled together on the bench before the pianoforte, not bothering to discard their garments.

She worked at the belt on his banyan. "I am afraid we have no recourse but to make up for our lost time."

"Ah, the woman who owns my heart." He peeled her from her dressing gown and shrugged the garment to the floor.

Naked, they made their way to the bed. Damian helped her settle into a comfortable position.

"I am terribly ungainly," she observed.

"You are wonderfully beautiful," he countered, kissing his way up her body.

He lingered over her belly, then settled between her thighs. Her body was in such a fervor that one swipe of his tongue over her pearl nearly had her spending. When he sank two fingers inside her and sucked on the sensitive bundle of flesh there at the same time, a delicious wave of bliss crashed over her.

He rose, aligning their bodies at the angle her condition would still allow, and slid deep. They sighed as one when he was seated fully within her throbbing sheath.

He paused, shifting so he could suckle her nipples before kissing her softly on the lips. "I love you, Mira."

"I love you, too, my wonderful man."

He moved, starting a rhythm that was steady and fast, so frenzied that she came again, tightening on his cock, her nails raking down his arms, careful to avoid the still-tender patch of flesh where he had recently required Gen, who Mirabel had learned was the secret owner of Lady Fortune, to ink him with the initials of their entire family. *MPJDG.* Mira, Percy, Joanna, Davy, Gideon, and soon one more would go there as well.

He thrust into her again before he stiffened, crying out as he filled her with his seed. The warm rush made her tingle with delicious reverberations of pleasure. When he collapsed at her side, she rolled into him, wrapping him in her arms.

"Do you remember that night when you told me to stay as

long as I liked? Stay forever, you said," she murmured. "I had never longed for something more in my life."

He nodded and kissed her crown, holding her every bit as tightly as she did him. "Nor I."

"Well." Smiling, she tipped back her head to take in his beloved face. "I think I shall accept your offer, Mr. Winter. I will stay forever."

"Damned right you will," he growled.

His lips found hers once more.

AUTHOR'S NOTE

Thank you so very much for reading *Winter's Widow*!

Please note that in this book, I intentionally left a bit of a mystery that still needs to be solved. What happened to Gavin, for instance? And who was Hugo's murderer? Why was Demon attacked? You'll have to read the next installment of The Wicked Winters series, *Winter's Warrior*, to find out! Read on for a sneak peek at Gavin Winter and Miss Caro Sutton's story.

Some notes on history before you head to that sneak peek:

The Natural History of Selborne (1788) by Gilbert White, was my companion for Gideon's knowledge of birds. I also drew inspiration for Octavia's favorite scandalous broadsides from Regency era caricaturists James Gillray and Thomas Rowlandson, among others. Once more, I owe Davy and Demon's cant and other wonderful turns of phrase to *The Memoirs of James Hardy Vaux* (1819) and Grose's *Dictionary of the Vulgar Tongue* (1811). In case you were wondering, the word *condom* has been in use in various forms for centuries (as has the condom itself), and is defined in *Dictionary of the Vulgar Tongue* using the spelling "cundum." I opted for the modern spelling in this book.

Now, what are you waiting for? Keep reading for more Wicked Winters in *Winter's Warrior*...

Until next time,
Scarlett

PREVIEW OF WINTER'S WARRIOR

THE WICKED WINTERS BOOK 13

Gavin Winter has earned his reputation as one of the best prizefighters in England the hard way: using his fists and sheer determination. With the biggest bout of his career approaching, Gavin will do anything to win.
Until he's attacked and wakes with no memory of who he is.

When Caro Sutton finds a bleeding man outside her family's gaming hell, she has no idea the felled giant is the bareknuckle champion. She nurses him back to health, charmed by the handsome gentleman who has no recollection of what happened to him or what his name is.

After she discovers his true identity, Caro is faced with a difficult choice. She must either reveal to him she is the sister of his enemy and risk losing Gavin forever, or preserve her secret and their blossoming romance.

Will deceit, danger, and warring families prove too much to overcome? Or will their love be strong enough to unite the Winters and the Suttons?

WINTER'S WARRIOR, PROLOGUE

EAST LONDON, 1815

It had taken three of her brother's guards to carry the felled giant from the streets and settle him in Caro's bed. But after he regained consciousness and began to fight, it had required five of them to help her tie the thrashing monster to the posts so she could tend him.

"Bloody madman," cautioned Randall as Caro secured the man's left wrist.

"Touched in the 'ead," counseled Hugh with a grunt as he narrowly escaped a swinging right fist before catching the man's arm and holding it to the post.

Good thing she was a bloody expert at securing prisoners. That was what spending her entire life in a gaming hell did to a girl. The beast would not escape a Caro Sutton knot.

"If he is mad, we will send him on his way," she promised, slipping around the bed to tie his other wrist as Bennet, Timothy, and Anthony held the man's legs.

"Sutton is going to rip out our guts and feed them to 'is dogs when 'e gets a sniff of this, miss." The warning, issued by Bennet, was an exaggeration.

Likely.

"I have never seen Jasper feeding entrails to his dogs yet," she said calmly, finishing the knot.

The man suddenly roared, half-insensate yet still struggling for his life.

She laid a gentle hand on his brow, which was matted with blood. "Calm yourself, sir. I only aim to help."

"I'll kill you," the man growled, thrashing some more.

It was impossible to tell if he was awake or in the grips of violent delirium. His eyes had swelled closed. The beating he had received had been merciless. There was the distinct possibility that he was also drunk, though she did not smell spirits on him. She had seen more than her share of sotted fools getting beaten and robbed in the alleys around The Sinner's Palace over the years. 'Twould be nothing new.

When she had first come across him in the alley behind her family's gaming hell, she had believed he was dead. A closer examination had proven otherwise; his chest had been rising and falling. That had been when she'd fetched Randall, Hugh, and Bennet. But from the moment she had first touched him, she had known instinctively there was something different about this man.

Her reluctant patient aimed another kick at Bennet and Timothy, landing a boot in the midst of the latter's abdomen. Timothy fell on his arse, clutching his belly and gasping for breath.

"Damn it," she grumbled.

Fortunately, she was accustomed to unruly men in need of healing. She tended to her brothers whenever there was a fight involving knives, fists, pistols, or sometimes all three at once—the Suttons were a bloodthirsty lot. There was no other solution when a man was out of his head as this one was. She was going to have to pour some laudanum down the poor cove's throat.

"Hold his head still for me, Randall," she ordered, fetching the bag she always kept at the ready and plucking the vial she required from it. "But take care where you touch him. We don't want to give him further injuries."

"If 'e bites me, I ain't going to be 'appy," the guard said.

A few months ago, her brother Rafe had accidentally bitten Randall's finger instead of the leather strip he'd been meant to gnaw on whilst she had stitched up a particularly vicious knife wound. Randall had not forgotten. Nor had he entirely forgiven Caro, even if he did favor her over all her siblings.

Caro did not fool herself for the reason. If the men were on the wrong end of a knife stick, they wanted to be certain she would be at their sides. The whispers circulating about her in the hell—that she could heal anyone—had not been aided by her natural inclination toward the medicinal. Nor all the treatises she spent each night reading until the stub of her candle flickered out.

"He shan't bite you," she told Randall, drawing nearer as the man continued to thrash and shout curses. "As long as your hold remains firm, that is."

Randall glared at her, but he did as she asked, dutifully holding her patient still as she held the vial to his lips and forced the laudanum into his mouth. Just to be certain he would swallow, for there was no telling with a man in his condition, she pinched his nostrils together. He made a choking sound but complied.

When she was satisfied he had swallowed enough of the liquid to calm him, she turned to the three men at his feet. "Hold him still for me, lads."

WINTER'S WARRIOR, CHAPTER 1

His only memories were of a vicious witch trying to kill him.

She had cast a spell over him, until he felt as if he were weighed down by boulders and had been unable to move. Then, she had forced a bittersweet potion down his throat until the darkness claimed him.

As he pondered it now, he was sure it had been the delirium of the fever Caro said had raged through him after she had found him, beaten nearly to death, with a pistol wound in his upper arm. Fortunately, the ball had passed cleanly through, but the infection that had set in after she'd stitched him up had almost been the end of him.

And the source of those terrible nightmares, which still clawed at him every night when he fell asleep.

But it was morning, light shining through the edges of the window dressings, and the bustle of the street below telling him it was past time to rise. His stomach growled, as if in competition with the din of the voices of the men and women and the clattering of drays passing in the street.

Hunger was a good sign. It meant his broken body was healing.

Too bad his mind continued to be utter rot.

He threw back the bedclothes and rose, shucking the nightshirt the glowering fellow named Randall had helped him to don the evening before following his bath. Removing the shirt required great care and patience, for his injured arm remained difficult to move. Now that he was at last feeling like a man instead of an invalid, however, it was worth the risk. He had been longing to wear the shirt and trousers which were neatly folded and awaiting him across the room.

When Caro had brought him the clothing a few days ago, he had not yet been strong enough to don them. But each day, he regained more of his ability. And when he had risen this morning, he had decided it was at last time to make an effort.

He may not recall a single, damned detail about who he was or why he had found himself nearly dead behind a gaming hell called The Sinner's Palace, but today, he was going to wear some cursed rigging as if he were an ordinary chap.

He winced as he struggled to remove his wounded arm from the sleeve of the nightshirt, then cried out as the stitches pulled. But he was determined. Biting his lip hard, he pulled his arm free, then slid the entire garment over his head.

The door to the chamber flew open and Caro stepped over the threshold, bearing a tray.

He froze, and the one portion of his anatomy which seemed to have remained unaffected by the injuries he had endured, went rigid. Forgetting himself, he attempted to clamp his hands over his cockstand, and howled in pain as the stitches in his arm pulled once more.

Wide, hazel eyes were upon him. Upon *that* particular part of him.

"Oh bloody hell," she said, bobbling the tray and nearly sending its contents to the floor. "Forgive me. I had no notion you were bare-arsed."

The heavy door had already closed on its own momentum at her back.

They were alone.

Damnation, she was beautiful. Through the haze of pain, through the agony of fire burning in his arm, he recognized it. The shock of the hasty movement of his arm had made his cock soften, but it did not remain so for long.

It never did in this woman's presence. Miss Caro Sutton was an angel. He was convinced of it.

Want more? Get *Winter's Warrior* now!

DON'T MISS SCARLETT'S OTHER ROMANCES!

Complete Book List
HISTORICAL ROMANCE

Heart's Temptation
A Mad Passion (Book One)
Rebel Love (Book Two)
Reckless Need (Book Three)
Sweet Scandal (Book Four)
Restless Rake (Book Five)
Darling Duke (Book Six)
The Night Before Scandal (Book Seven)

Wicked Husbands
Her Errant Earl (Book One)
Her Lovestruck Lord (Book Two)
Her Reformed Rake (Book Three)
Her Deceptive Duke (Book Four)
Her Missing Marquess (Book Five)
Her Virtuous Viscount (Book Six)

DON'T MISS SCARLETT'S OTHER ROMANCES!

League of Dukes
Nobody's Duke (Book One)
Heartless Duke (Book Two)
Dangerous Duke (Book Three)
Shameless Duke (Book Four)
Scandalous Duke (Book Five)
Fearless Duke (Book Six)

Notorious Ladies of London
Lady Ruthless (Book One)
Lady Wallflower (Book Two)
Lady Reckless (Book Three)
Lady Wicked (Book Four)
Lady Lawless (Book Five)

The Wicked Winters
Wicked in Winter (Book One)
Wedded in Winter (Book Two)
Wanton in Winter (Book Three)
Wishes in Winter (Book 3.5)
Willful in Winter (Book Four)
Wagered in Winter (Book Five)
Wild in Winter (Book Six)
Wooed in Winter (Book Seven)
Winter's Wallflower (Book Eight)
Winter's Woman (Book Nine)
Winter's Whispers (Book Ten)
Winter's Waltz (Book Eleven)
Winter's Widow (Book Twelve)
Winter's Warrior (Book Thirteen)

Stand-alone Novella
Lord of Pirates

DON'T MISS SCARLETT'S OTHER ROMANCES!

CONTEMPORARY ROMANCE

Love's Second Chance
Reprieve (Book One)
Perfect Persuasion (Book Two)
Win My Love (Book Three)

Coastal Heat
Loved Up (Book One)

ABOUT THE AUTHOR

USA Today and Amazon bestselling author Scarlett Scott writes steamy Victorian and Regency romance with strong, intelligent heroines and sexy alpha heroes. She lives in Pennsylvania and Maryland with her Canadian husband, adorable identical twins, and one TV-loving dog.

A self-professed literary junkie and nerd, she loves reading anything, but especially romance novels, poetry, and Middle English verse. Catch up with her on her website http://www.scarlettscottauthor.com/. Hearing from readers never fails to make her day.

Scarlett's complete book list and information about upcoming releases can be found at http://www.scarlettscottauthor.com/.

Connect with Scarlett! You can find her here:
Join Scarlett Scott's reader's group on Facebook for early excerpts, giveaways, and a whole lot of fun!
Sign up for her newsletter here.
Follow Scarlett on Amazon
Follow Scarlett on BookBub
www.instagram.com/scarlettscottauthor/
www.twitter.com/scarscoromance
www.pinterest.com/scarlettscott
www.facebook.com/AuthorScarlettScott

Printed in Dunstable, United Kingdom